LUCAS

The K9 Files, Book 5

Dale Mayer

LUCAS: THE K9 FILES, BOOK 5
Beverly Dale Mayer
Valley Publishing Ltd.

ISBN-13: 978-1-773361-89-5
Print Edition

Books in This Series

Dedication

It takes an army to make a book like this one, and that army also needs love and attention. Often it comes in the form of a furry friend. This book is dedicated to Lionel, a beloved pet of one of my beta readers who's worked with me for years. Lionel went to the wonderful cat home in the sky this last week and he'll be sorely missed.

Thanks for being such a devoted friend while here on earth! You'll be sorely missed.

About This Book

Welcome to the all new K9 Files series reconnecting readers with the unforgettable men from SEALs of Steel in a new series of action packed, page turning romantic suspense that fans have come to expect from USA TODAY Bestselling author Dale Mayer. Pssst... you'll meet other favorite characters from SEALs of Honor and Heroes for Hire too!

The world of dogfighting is an ugly place ...

When Tophat, a missing K9 dog, is accidentally sent to Canada as part of a group of rescued dogs looking for adoption, Lucas knows he's the natural pick for this job. Plus he has another reason to be in the country. His sister lives there, and ... so does his ex-fiancée.

But when he arrives, Lucas finds Tophat was handed over to a trainer who deals with aggressive dogs. The news isn't good, especially after Lucas arrives at the trainer's property and is thrown into the dark underworld of dogfighting.

Tanya used to share her home with her two best friends, until one was killed in a hit-and-run and the other badly injured. Now living alone in a small apartment, Tanya realizes how much she's lost—including Lucas. Unexpectedly seeing him flips her world once more ...

As Lucas digs deeper into Tophat's disappearance, the dogfighting ring rises up to protect their own ...

Sign up to be notified of all Dale's releases here!

https://geni.us/DaleNews

PROLOGUE

G EIR SAT DOWN in the boardroom beside Jager and Badger. "Well, that appears to have been a success," he said. "I just heard through the grapevine that Blaze has found Solo."

"Not only found Solo," Jager said with a chuckle, "but he also found a woman named Camilla, and apparently, we're having almost as much luck with our team's relationships as Levi and Mason are with theirs."

"I didn't expect to become a matchmaking service," Badger said, "but, with Kat around, it's hard not to be."

"She does want to see everybody as happy as she is," Geir said. "And that's kudos to you."

"No. I think it's kudos to all of us," Badger said. "So, four War Dogs are all good, eight more to go. Anybody got any suggestions about who or where next?"

"I was flipping through these files," Geir said. "The dogs are all over the place."

"That'll make it more difficult," Jager said. "So far we've been picking dogs that matched men and where they needed to be. I didn't tell Blaze that I knew about his need to return to Kentucky, but, when I saw the dog was from that same area, I figured that was a perfect match. But I don't know of any other matches."

Geir shuffled through the files, picked up one, and said.

"Top Hat. Love that name." The file photo revealed a shepherd with lighter coloring, but his neck was all dark, like he wore an ascot. While impressive in size, those expressive eyes were filled with life. He smiled as he looked at it and tapped the photo. "Every time I look at that pic, I think that guy has got to be in a circus or something."

"Hardly. From what I heard, Top Hat had an aggressive tendency that was hard to control," Badger said. "He's the one that worries me because chances are he's been put down already."

"I don't know about that," Geir said. "I think these dogs are survivors. They've handled a lot. I can't imagine they'll give up now."

"Maybe not give up," Jager said, "but it doesn't mean it'll be easy for them to adapt to civilian life. We need the right person for this one."

"Top Hat's in Canada. He was somehow shipped with a large group of rescue dogs to Alberta," Badger said with a shake of his head.

"Which is miles and miles of a whole lot of nothing. A couple big cities and lots of small towns. With farmers in between. Or is that Saskatchewan? Whatever," Geir said. "Besides, just because Top Hat ended up in Alberta doesn't mean he's still there."

"That's true enough," Badger said. "We can attempt to uncover more intel, but do we know anybody with connections up there that could cut through a lot of that random research and footwork?"

"Lucas does," Geir said. "His sister married a Canadian."

"So it might be time for him to have a family visit."

"But let's get real," Jager joked. "Canada is massive, and just because some guy's sister married a Canadian doesn't mean the dog is anywhere close by."

"No. Not at all," Badger agreed. "But it also doesn't mean it isn't time for Lucas to visit his sister, and, in the meantime, we'll get some intel and try to find out where the dog ended up." Badger looked at Geir, who just grinned broadly at them. "Okay, Geir. What do you know that we don't?"

"Lucas's sister is in Medicine Hat, Alberta," he said. "She married the son of a farmer."

"See? What did I tell you?" Jager said, rolling his eyes.

"It doesn't mean Lucas wants to go home and doesn't mean Lucas even gives a damn about dogs," Jager added.

"No, maybe not, but he was search and rescue for years. The whole family is heavily involved in it. I think his father used to train search and rescue dogs."

"Wow," Badger said, rubbing his hands together. "It sounds like we have our next success story."

"Is he married?" Jager asked. "Because that will completely change things."

"Was engaged," Geir replied. "Something blew up between the two of them, and they separated. I know it's been eating at him for months and months. She lives close to his sister. The two are friends."

"Oh, interesting," Badger said. "Even more reason for him to return and settle this—either to break free or to get back together with her."

"I don't think getting back together is an option," Geir said, "but one never knows."

"What do you guys think? Should we try it?"

"Why not? Let's bring him in, and see what he thinks."

CHAPTER 1

L UCAS SCOTT HAD used lesser excuses to head up to visit his sister and brother-in-law, but this was the weirdest. Here he would be searching for a K9 military dog, a former War Dog, that had somehow been caught up in a group of rescue dogs and shipped to Canada.

He never really understood how that worked, but his research had pinpointed the fact that hundreds of rescue dogs were taken to Canada for adoption as they had a better reception up there than down South. It bothered him to a certain extent because he'd like to think of his people taking care of their own animals. However, when it came to a War Dog being a rescue, and one unlikely to be adopted in his own country, even after all the dog had done to keep his own country safe—well, that wasn't cool, and, from what Lucas heard, the dog was unstable and potentially dangerous.

Yet, he immediately focused on the picture in the file. *That* dog was not unstable and dangerous. Lucas could see it in his eyes. Even in a photo. So how in the hell could someone in their right mind see that dog in real life and deem him unstable? Lucas shook his head.

That could also be the handlers' problems. These War Dogs were impeccably trained, but not everyone knew how to handle them.

Top Hat had been a strong military dog but had taken a

turn for the worse after a mission where he'd been attacked and badly wounded. Lucas felt an instant tie to the dog on this fact alone. Top Hat's physical wounds had healed, but his temperament, although better, wasn't the same. He was no longer the amiable soul he'd been before.

And that was just a bad mix for everybody.

Yet, just one look into Top Hot's expressive eyes—even in a two-dimensional photo—and Lucas *knew*. Lucas knew this War Dog had been one hell of a soldier. But those dark-chocolate-colored eyes? A puppy still lived in there.

No one seemed to know how Top Hat was doing. Lucas contacted the Fur & Feather Rescue Shelter, and they had confirmed they had the dog there. But they hadn't said much else. Lucas fought a losing battle trying to get some straight answers here. Hell, any answers. When he tried to explain the history of the dog, they had laughed and said they didn't think that could be correct. Otherwise, why would the dog have ended up in their yard?

He'd asked them to check for tattoos, and they had told Lucas how hard it was to get close to Top Hat. He was on a warning list, and they were hoping somebody with skills to handle the more difficult dog would take him on as a foster animal and could calm him down, with the ultimate goal being that he'd eventually be placed for adoption.

Lucas told them that he would be there in four days, since he was flying to see a friend on the US side of the border, then traveling the rest of the way in his truck. They acknowledged it, but that had been the end of it. Lucas did not appreciate their apathetic response to him or to Top Hat. If people didn't love and respect animals, what the hell were they doing working in an animal shelter? Lucas shook his head, trying to stop the anger building in him.

Since he'd gotten on the road, he had once again contacted the Fur & Feather Rescue Shelter, just to confirm he was on the way. They had passed the dog along to another shelter, the Red Deer Rescue Shelter. When Lucas heard that, he hung up on them. He had no time to deal with them, but he would have liked to get his hands wrapped about the neck of the person in charge back there. Yet, Lucas couldn't waste his energy on them. Lucas had to focus on Top Hat. And on himself for that matter.

Already just a short jog into his drive, Lucas figured Top Hat was in trouble. Lucas didn't know what it was, but an inkling inside him said that something was wrong. Very wrong. Seriously wrong. His gut stayed knotted the whole way. Was it about Lucas's frustrations from the very beginning in his search for Top Hat? Or was that because it was his first long road trip since he'd been injured? Or was it all about Tanya—his ex-fiancée? The only woman he'd loved enough to ask to marry him? And still the only woman he'd ever loved.

Or all of the above? *Probably.*

Normally he wouldn't drive either—at least not since his accident—but, for some reason, it seemed like he needed his own wheels. And maybe it was a chance to check out his ability to handle the drive again. He'd left his truck with a buddy who'd planned to buy it off him, but then the guy had changed his mind. The buddy and Lucas's truck were both in Glacier National Park in Montana's Rocky Mountains, so he'd flown in to see his buddy and to retrieve his truck, then had driven across the border into Alberta, Canada, to see his sister.

Which was silly. It probably would have been cheaper to fly the whole way. Still, if he was bringing Top Hat back to the US, he had to have a way to get him home. They could have possibly flown but that hadn't seemed like the answer at the time. Lucas worried about a quarantine period of whatever length when flying back into the States and about stressing out the dog further with an airplane ride. Lucas never checked it out now that he had wheels. For that matter, he still needed to research what was entailed in bringing a dog from Canada and crossing the border back into the States. He hoped a veterinarian's bill of good health was enough. He'd find out more about that later.

Maybe some things just had to happen in the way they had to happen.

Besides, the trip itself was going decently. He was pleasantly surprised. And feeling a little triumphant if he were honest with himself. He'd just crossed the border at Sweet Grass, Montana, into the Alberta region of Canada, and was not more than two hours away from his sister's place in Medicine Hat. The latest shelter where Top Hat had been taken was four hours from his sister's place.

As he pulled up to his sister's house, relieved that his first physical test of this kind was over, Meg came out the front door, a big smile on her face.

He grinned as he parked his truck and slid out slowly. "Good to see you, sis."

She didn't say a word but threw her arms around his chest and gave him a big hug.

He was six-four; she was five-six, and the difference was even more obvious now. She'd had two kids, and, instead of growing bigger, she'd shrunk. He swore she was down to five-four now.

"What happened? You shrink with the last one?"

"Or the stress since having a baby, especially since it was

the second one," she admitted. "You look like you've done nothing but grow."

"I have," he said. "But hopefully in good ways."

She pulled back, looked at the muscle on his chest and shoulders, smiled and said, "You certainly haven't lost any of the muscle."

"I have," he replied. "But mostly along the back. And I've worked damn hard to get back the muscle I lost."

Her smile dipped. "Right, we won't ever forget that you broke your back, lost two ribs and one kidney and ... more."

"Maybe," he said quietly, "but we don't need to dwell on it either."

She smiled again, sending a ray of sunshine everywhere.

He shook his head. "Damn, I've missed that smile. You could take a dark day and turn it into one of the best with just the curve of your lips."

"Ha!" she said with a toss of her head, sending the loose tendrils of hair flying around her face. "I doubt it. Come on in. The rest of the family is otherwise occupied."

He slid her a sideways look and raised an eyebrow. She laughed and said, "You'll find out."

He grabbed his bag from the bed of the truck and rotated his shoulders to ease some of the stress in his neck and followed her inside. He had a back cushion he used for long drives that gave him extra support. He'd done this drive home many times over his years as a SEAL, just not since his accident. He already knew his back muscles would seize in the morning. He swore softly as he felt a sudden jab in his spine. He'd have to be careful for the next few days that he didn't pull something. And to remember his stretches before bed. Then again he had already been slipping with that routine.

Meg shot him a questioning look, and then worry replaced the curiosity on her face. "Are you okay?"

He nodded and smiled. "Just a few twinges from the long ride."

"You could have flown," she said.

"I could've," he said, "but I didn't want to."

"You didn't drive all the way from New Mexico, did you?"

He shook his head. "Bronson has been hanging on to my truck in Montana for the last few months."

"I'm surprised you let him have it."

"He was going to buy it off me, but his mom gifted him with one. Since then my truck has been parked." He glanced at his black double-cab three-quarter-ton truck, damn glad to have it back. "I didn't think it would work for me after my surgeries, but I'm happy to say the trip was decent."

"Having it at his place helped this time," she said. "At least you got to cut the trip up—flew for part of it and then you got to drive the last few hours."

"If I didn't have this odd feeling that I needed my truck here, I probably would have flown all the way."

"I think it's better to have your independence," she said. "Besides, now you have your truck back, and I know you love that thing."

"I agree," he said. "Feels better to have my wheels, and you're right. I do love it."

Then she added, "But whatever is best for your back is what we want."

Once inside, he toed off his boots, dropped his bag and slipped out of his vest.

With a finger to her lips, she led him to the family room around the corner. There he watched his two nephews—

three-year-old Yegg and five-year-old Jonah—and Nathan, their father, playing Mario Kart on a game system on the TV. There were shrieks of laughter as they raced ahead of each other on the TV screen. Jonah was whipping their dad pretty darn good. When Jonah won, he stood up and tossed himself at his father, screaming, "I won! I won! I won!" Nathan rolled over, letting Yegg come and pounce on him too.

Lucas loved this glimpse and all the others he had had into their family life. A healthy, loving relationship all around. Not that they all didn't have their moments or their arguments. But there was no yelling here. Well, maybe to celebrate a win at Mario Kart, but no raising of voices to inhibit a real conversation about a real problem. He was so proud of his sister, what she and Nathan had built here.

It was *the* one thing he wanted for himself. His greatest desire. Always had been. Always would be. Even faced with the choice of having Tanya or having a family, Lucas knew what he had to do. He had to let her go. He had to find someone who wanted a family just as much as he did. He had wanted that someone to be Tanya.

He still did.

But the whole family issue had been the sole cause behind his breakup with Tanya. He hated to admit it, but it seemed like he was still waiting for Tanya to come to her senses and to call him again and to say that she now wanted a family as much as she wanted him. In his emotional moments he wondered if that would be a good thing or bad.

His sister called out, "Hey. You two want to say hi to your uncle?"

The two boys looked up, and Jonah squealed and raced for Lucas.

Lucas squatted down, careful of the weight hurtling toward him, even while overhearing his sister's cry, "Wait, Jonah. Wait." Lucas caught him easily, using his legs as he'd learned and straightened up, swinging the little boy around. Jonah squeezed his arms tight around Lucas's neck and hung on.

For a moment, Lucas buried his face into the hair of the innocent child in his arms and hung on. For a long time, he thought he'd never see this little guy again. It was such a relief to realize he was actually whole and back with his family. During his convalescence they'd shared FaceTime often, but that wasn't the same as holding this little body in his arms.

Meg reached out and gripped his wrist and said, "It's good to have you back."

He smiled at her over Jonah's head and whispered, "Thank you."

Nathan stretched a hand out, smacking him lightly on the shoulder. "Good to see you back, Lucas."

"Good to be back," he admitted. "Wasn't sure I'd make it."

"Neither were we," Meg said softly. "Jonah, let Uncle Lucas visit with Momma in the kitchen."

Jonah shook his head and refused to let Lucas go.

Chuckling, Lucas walked in and sat down at the kitchen table, trying to be careful with his back after the long trip. It didn't take much these days to jerk it into a full-blown problem again. He'd done a ton of rehab work and built up as much of the back muscles as he could. But he knew he would always have to watch out for his back now.

Jonah lifted his head and smiled the sweetest of smiles and said, "I'm glad you're alive."

And Lucas felt his heart melt.

He touched Jonah under the chin gently and said, "So am I, little man. So am I." And felt another little one leaning against his knee. Lucas reached a hand down, patting the child on the face, and said, "Hey, Eggy. How you doing?"

Their littlest boy beamed up at him—displaying all his baby teeth, which he was obviously proud of—and, with a fine dusting of hair, he was just adorable. Jonah scrambled off Lucas's lap and ran over to his mom and dad while Lucas greeted little Eggy. It was his nickname because he never ran in a straight line; instead he always went in sharp circles. His real name was Yegg, which was odd enough, but it was Nathan's grandfather's name, so everybody seemed to be okay with it.

He hugged Eggy and stroked the plump cheek with his other hand. There was just something special about a homecoming like this. His sister caught his eye and smiled. "You could live here, you know? I know it's not home for you yet, but it could be."

He gave his nephew an extra squeeze and then reached over and hugged his sister. "I'm here now," he said in a low voice. Breaking off his engagement had been hard on his sister too. She'd been ecstatic to think he'd be living close to her, finally. His accident, his injuries, his recovery, ... he often forgot it wasn't just him who'd gone through a lot. ... "That's what counts."

"Maybe," she said. "That was one of the most oddball reasons I've heard yet for coming home though. A dog? You know you don't need an excuse, right?"

He chuckled. "Hey, I've been home many times over the years when I had leave for no other reason than to see you. Sure, they weren't the easiest trips, but I did come."

"Yes," she said. "And this time you're after a dog?"

His brother-in-law turned and looked at him. "Yeah. I don't get that," he said. "Why this dog?"

Lucas tried to explain as much as he understood. "I just know that Top Hat apparently also has some behavioral issues after he was attacked by several other dogs, and the military is worried about him."

"Not other War Dogs, right?" Nathan asked.

Lucas shook his head. "I don't have all the details still. But, from what I've learned to date, Top Hat was initially wounded in the mission, a gunshot from all accounts. His blood drew in a pack of wild dogs in the area, which are all over Iraq. Of course his team came to his rescue, but Top Hat was already weak before the added attack, and he surely didn't understand these wild dogs compared to the War Dogs that Top Hat normally worked with."

"The poor thing," Meg said.

"So the military is worried about him or worried about those humans who might come in contact with him?" Nathan asked shrewdly. "Because, if it's a case of Top Hat needing some training, that's a different story, but, if he's aggressive and dangerous to families, we don't want him in a rescue center to be adopted by some unsuspecting mom and dad with young kids."

"I already contacted the center. The second one now. They do still have him, and I'm on my way to get him tomorrow," Lucas said. "Of course we have to do some paperwork to get him back across the border again."

"Right," Nathan said. "That's your problem. Although I'm surprised you're handling this. Isn't that the War Dogs Department's problem?"

"Well, it would have been, but that entire department

has been disbanded. Titanium Corp was asked to look into these last few cases of lost War Dogs, hoping they've ended up in good homes. And my friends at Titanium asked me to have a look into this dog's situation."

"Fine. But if he's super-aggressive," Nathan continued, "that'll cause problems no matter which side of the border he's on."

Lucas nodded. "That's tomorrow's problem. I have to see what shape he's in and then report back first."

His sister clapped her hands and said, "Okay. Let's have dinner."

TANYA NOLAN ANSWERED her phone, surprised to see Meg's name come up on her Caller ID. They had just talked first thing this morning. "Hey, Meg. What's up?"

"Lucas is here," Meg said abruptly. "I don't know if that's a good thing or a bad thing for you, but I didn't want you coming over unexpectedly, and the two of you having an argument."

At the news, all Tanya could do was suck back her breath. "Why is he here?" she asked bluntly. She hated there was that eternal hope in the back of her mind. That maybe, just maybe, he had come back to see her.

"He's on a mission of some sort involving a dog," Meg replied. "Even though it seems odd, it is a legitimate job. We did quiz him about it, but apparently a War Dog was accidentally shipped up here, and so Lucas is heading out to the center tomorrow to check it out."

"For real?" Tanya had a hard time with that as an excuse. But, then again, he hadn't shown any inclination to come see her again. Neither had she called him. Not recently anyway. Their breakup had been bad. Painful. Awful. Then she'd heard about his accident and injuries. She had tried to get in touch with him then, but he wouldn't answer her calls.

He'd been up here twice since their breakup—once before his accident and now this one—and she'd yet to see him. She didn't know how bad the damage was, although Meg kept telling her how Lucas was doing fine. Tanya knew he wasn't fine because he'd spent six months in a hospital. He had broken his back and lost several ribs. She really wanted to see that he was "fine" with her own two eyes. She didn't know what else had gone on with him, other than Meg's generic updates, but Tanya knew that, when Lucas was down and out, she had tried to get in touch with him, but he didn't want anything to do with her.

That had hurt in a big way.

She understood, but, at the same time, it was devastating. She still loved him, always had. She didn't necessarily want to marry him anymore because they had such divergent plans for their future—she didn't want a family, and he did—and that was one of those essential cores to a marriage, where a successful marriage needed the parties to be aligned, either both pro or both con. But she hadn't changed her mind. Yet, it hadn't changed how she felt about him either.

Had he changed how he felt about her?

She had no idea. Well, she had an idea and dismissed it.

Had he changed about wanting a family? Chances were high that he hadn't. Family was very important to him. He adored Meg's boys. Always had. He'd always wanted a big family. But, for her, well, that was the last thing she wanted, and, for that, she felt guilty as hell. She had raised her younger siblings like some single mother, when their real mom was alive and always working. The maternal responsibilities had fallen on Tanya's shoulders and had cured her of wanting to raise more. She felt like she'd been there and done that.

Everybody kept telling her it would be different when it was her own child, yet she hadn't any inclination to get pregnant to prove that theory. The last thing she wanted to do, if she ever would be a mother, was to be a terrible one, like her own mother, and that was all she could think she'd be.

She had choices now that she had left her mother behind to deal with her children herself. One of the hardest choices since then had been to break up with Lucas because he had wanted a family. He'd been angry when he had heard her reasoning. But, when she asked him if he was prepared to go through life without children, and he had told her no, she had told him that they had no future.

As she put down the phone, she thought about all the things that had happened since she'd broken it off with Lucas. All the things he'd gone through, and all the things she'd gone through.

She'd lost her job and picked up several small useless jobs until she had landed her current job and had done a whole lot of introspection, taking another look at her life. Before that she'd also lost her roommates—one had been murdered, and the other was in a drug-induced coma after a car accident. The families had come and moved out both girls' possessions, and Tanya was left with monthly bills that, once she lost her job, she could not afford on her own, so she had moved to a small one-bedroom apartment.

She didn't really like how things were going, but she didn't know how to fix it. It was as if, since breaking off with

Lucas, the universe had decided to show her exactly what her life without him was like. And she didn't think much of it. Now she stood all alone, wondering what the hell was going on.

She worked as a cashier in a department store, ringing up purchases for customers, even though she was an accountant. At her previous job, somebody had said she was stealing from her employer, and there had been a horrible inquiry that had made her feel like she was a thief, even though she wasn't. She had no clue who reported her, but she had lost her job regardless of later proof she was not at fault. The boss had said the trust factor had been broken.

It wasn't that the company didn't trust her, her boss had said, but they didn't trust anybody anymore.

For her, that had been devastating because it had been a good paying job. Getting laid off had come with incredibly difficult consequences, and, in this small community where she lived, that led to dire consequences. One of which was, she couldn't get another job in her field since then.

It broke her heart to see how her life had gone from one extreme to the other. She couldn't overlook that she had it better than her two friends, but it was a far cry from how Tanya's life had been with Lucas.

Most evenings she spent time at Alice's bedside. But it was hard because her friend was practically vegetative. Tanya knew Alice was in there and that she would heal—the doctors said so—but the process was slow. That was the whole point of going—connecting to her friend and letting her friend know she was there. While, at the same time, Tanya herself had nothing to look forward to except for the future hope that her friend wake up.

As for Claire, her other friend who had died, Tanya took

a walk every weekend to Claire's grave, where Tanya would sit and think of nothing more than the fact that this beautiful young woman had been cut down in the prime of her life. Sometimes, when Tanya got really depressed, she wondered if it didn't have to do with her breaking up with Lucas. Because it seemed like that was the point when everything went south.

She'd never considered such a thing as karma and fate before, but, since losing Lucas and then Claire and then Alice, Tanya had done a ton of thinking about it. She had had viable reasons for breaking up with Lucas, so she didn't understand why that would cause everything else to go to hell. Her other friends at work had laughed at her when she had told them what she'd done.

Her mother had said Tanya was a fool. But then her mother had never understood what life had been like for the eldest of the seven children when their mother was too busy working and having multiple boyfriends to spend any time with her children.

Tanya felt bad for even complaining because her mother still managed to provide a roof over their heads while keeping all seven children. None were shipped off to a shelter. But her mother never learned about birth control either. All that hadn't been fun, and Tanya didn't want to do it again now, even though her four sisters were grown up with lives of their own. Not the youngest boys though. They were still at home and likely would be for a few more years yet. Tanya couldn't even remember exactly how old they were anymore.

She felt like she'd been robbed of her childhood and now robbed of motherhood.

She sat here wondering what she should do. Should she

try to see Lucas? With everything going on in her life and with life being so short for Claire and Alice, maybe that was exactly what Tanya needed to do. Lucas would be at the shelter in the morning. She thought it was maybe a four hour drive away—eight hours or more round trip. The more she thought about it, she wondered if maybe he wanted company for the trip. She picked up her phone and called Meg back.

As soon as Meg answered, Tanya said, "May I speak to Lucas, please?"

Meg paused, and Tanya kept her voice calm and neutral. "It won't hurt to talk to him, will it?"

Meg sighed. "No. It won't. But I don't want him upset," she warned. "He spent a lot of time recovering."

"Will talking to me send him in a tailspin?" She hated to even think of it. But she couldn't blame Meg. If it was one of her siblings, Tanya would have asked the same questions.

Meg groaned and asked her friend to hang on. In the background Tanya could hear her calling her brother.

They had a muffled conversation, as if Meg had put her hand over the mouthpiece. That was too damn bad because it would be nice to know his reaction. To know if Lucas hated her for what she'd done.

"Hello, Tanya. What's up?"

She stared at the phone, surprised. How could he be so calm and so neutral? There wasn't even a strain to his voice when she was sitting here on tenterhooks. "Meg says you're driving the long trip up to the rescue center. Is that correct?"

"Yes," he replied cautiously. "Why?"

"I have the day off," she said abruptly. "Are you up for company for the drive?"

CHAPTER 2

S HE WAITED NERVOUSLY outside her apartment the next
morning at seven. It was early, but they had nearly a
four-hour drive ahead of them.

He pulled up on time. That was Lucas. He was someone
you could count on all the time. So why the hell had she not
figured out that was important? And although they had some
big differences, they were her issues, not his. He was perfect.
Always had been. Now if only she could figure out how to
walk time back and regain all they'd lost.

If he didn't already have anyone new.

She hopped in. "Thank you for letting me come." She
feasted her eyes on him, loving the way that one wayward
front lock of hair resisted going with the flow and always
hung slightly off center. With a little curl to the rich brown
color, it had always looked perfect.

He gave a clipped nod.

She looked for an opening to break the ice. Taking a
deep breath, she said in a bright voice, "So … why is this dog
important?"

He gave a brief explanation. When he was done, he
glanced at her before asking, "After all this time why did you
want to come with me?"

"I wanted to see you," she said bluntly. "You've been out
twice before and avoided me."

"I came up to visit family before," he said equally as blunt. "And I wasn't ready to see you."

She sighed heavily. "Why didn't you take my calls?"

"What calls?" he asked, frowning, glancing at her again.

He really didn't remember? She shook her head. "I called—twice—while you were in the hospital. As soon as I heard from Meg what had happened to you, I just needed to hear to your voice." She glanced at him, gauging his reaction. His face was one big grimace. That couldn't be good. "Why didn't you take my calls?"

Lucas gave his own heavy sigh. Then seemed to be counting to ten. Finally he spoke. "You know how I get when I'm sick. That hasn't changed." He stared at her to say the next few words. "*I* haven't changed." He shook his head, watching the road again. "I just want to sleep, give my body a couple days to focus solely on healing. Like a bear hibernating, I just need to be left alone. And I'm a grumpy bear if anybody interrupts my hibernation."

She wondered if this was such a good idea after all to be trapped in an all-day road trip with Lucas.

"But, Lucas," she said, getting his attention, at least briefly, "this wasn't two days to get over the flu. You were attacked. It took months of surgeries and rehab."

He frowned at her, seemed surprised that she knew.

"Meg and I have always been close. She keeps me up-to-date on what's going on in your life."

Lucas immediately turned away and stared out the side window, then faced the roadway, but ... not her.

"Does that bother you?"

His shoulders visibly relaxed. Then he shook his head, but it was such a minute movement that she almost missed it. "I'm glad you and Meg are close."

He wasn't normally so blunt, nor so uncaring of her feelings. But she needed the honesty. She knew he'd taken the breakup hard.

"Sorry," he said. "I don't mean to be mean."

"You never mean to be," she said. "Sometimes we have to be mean to those we love to get them to understand." He didn't say anything. She smiled. "Anyway, thank you for letting me come. Otherwise, I'd be sitting at home doing nothing and hating my life."

"Why?" he asked. "What's been going on?"

"You sure you want to hear?" she asked with a broken laugh. "Remember Alice and Claire?"

He nodded. "Of course. The three of you were *The Three Musketeers*."

"Well, Claire is dead. Alice is in the hospital in a coma." She wrapped her arms around herself, as if trying hard to hide her grief. "Claire was murdered."

"Jesus," he said softly. "Seriously?"

She nodded. "The RCMP have some leads but haven't found out who killed her yet."

"Any idea how she was killed?"

"She was kidnapped on her way home from work one day. She decided she should walk home. Then that was her. She loved to jog and walk—she was very much the outdoor girl. She never made it home. Her body was found two days later."

"How did she die?"

Tanya sighed. "It's horrible."

"Stabbed? Shot? Strangled?"

"Looked like a dog attack," she said, her voice breaking up despite her best efforts to control it. "Her throat was ripped out, and she had bite marks all over her body."

The cab of the truck was eerily quiet. She shouldn't have been so graphic, but it was an image she couldn't get out of her mind.

"Dogs?" he asked quietly. "Are we talking about dog-fights?"

"The police are looking at that angle because we have had some problems recently with underground dogfighting rings. The police rescued dozens of dogs. At least two of them had to be put down because they couldn't be saved."

"Did Claire have anything to do with any of the people involved in those cases?"

"Who knows?" she said. "She was one of the dispatchers for the RCMP, so it's possible."

"That's rough," he said. "I'm sorry."

"I am too. It's been a rough few months."

"How long ago did this happen?"

"One hundred and twenty-six days ago." The number fell off her tongue because she'd been counting every day.

"What happened to Alice?" he asked, looking at her.

She glanced at him and then out the front windshield. He had the softest gray eyes. They still had the same impact on her.

She sighed. "She was hit by a car crossing the road, and the driver fled the scene."

"And let me guess. The police never caught who did it?" he asked drily.

"No. But then I'm not sure I can blame them. It was nighttime. She left a bar, at night, dressed in black ... At least she's alive, and she will recover, but she'll be in the hospital for a while."

"Do you get to see her?"

"I go a lot. Unfortunately that has also become a bit of a

crutch as I'm either sitting at Claire's graveside or sitting at Alice's bedside. A lot of people think it's not very healthy. I can't walk away though. I'm just so angry, and I feel shitty that I'm the only one left."

"Being a survivor can be a terrible guilt trip."

She stared at him, her lips parting in surprise. But what he said made an odd kind of sense. "Oh. ... Survivor's guilt? Yes. ... You're right. I hadn't thought of it that way. But that's what it is. I feel guilty because I'm okay, and they aren't."

AS LUCAS HAD already considered over and over again earlier this morning, he wondered at the impulse to allow Tanya to accompany him. He'd avoided talking to her all this time, but the request had come out of the blue.

It was one thing to have the company of somebody you really liked; it was another thing to have the company of somebody you really loved and had broken up with you. Then add in the passage of time and the lack of communication, and you wondered if you were friends at this point or not ever again. Maybe that was why he was doing this. To see if they were still friends. Or at least had the hope to be friends one day. He didn't know, but the impulse to say yes to Tanya had been strong.

He knew his sister had been surprised, and he also knew he'd shocked Tanya because there'd been nothing but silence at the other end of the phone initially. Then she'd hurriedly asked him what time she should be ready, and, after he had told her, she'd rung off, and that had been it.

Until now. Except he hadn't slept well thinking about

her, worrying at the pain of leaving her again. It had taken him weeks if not months to get over their breakup—and, in truth, he never did. He carried this sense of being suspended in time—waiting for them to pick up where they'd left off.

A part of him had thought she'd chicken out and not show up this morning, but he hadn't been able to hope that she'd be true to her word. He couldn't wait to see her again. It was all he could think about, and surprise—not really— she'd been there, looking nervous and still gorgeous. Dressed in jeans with a simple white T-shirt and sweater, her long blond hair pulled back into a ponytail. She'd always had a fresh innocence about her, such a casual beauty, as if she were completely unaware of how beautiful she was …

He'd always known it. She was sincerely gorgeous inside too. But she had one issue which she had let dominate her future. It was what had broken them up. … And it was a big one.

She didn't look any different except a little older, a little like life hadn't been easy on her the last few months, but then it hadn't been easy on him either. Although what had happened to her two girlfriends …

He couldn't believe what he had heard. "They were both so full of life," he said. "It's hard to imagine they've been stopped in their tracks like that."

"At least in Alice's case," she said quietly, "it's not permanent."

"Were the incidences connected?"

She shook her head.

He studied her for a long moment. "Are you sure?"

"I don't think so," she said. "They were as different as can be."

"Maybe, but if anybody knew they were very good

friends, maybe somebody was worried they had seen something they shouldn't have or that they discussed something they shouldn't have."

"Then they obviously didn't know Claire. She never said anything to anybody about anything," Tanya said firmly. "She never discussed any part of her work."

"Some jobs are like that," he said. "But somebody might have thought she'd have shared with her best friends."

"Besides, if that were the case, they would have come after me too."

"Maybe ..." he said. "Have you noticed anybody watching you or hanging around?"

"No," she said. "But then again I moved, and I doubt anybody knows where I live now. I couldn't afford the old place, not on my own, not after everything that happened."

He thought about that for a moment. "You mean, after the girls couldn't contribute their share of the rent?"

"That was definitely a big part of it. I probably could have hung on, but then I lost my job," she said quietly. "For a while I worked at several dead-end jobs for minimum wage, more than one at the same time, until I ended up with the one I have now, which isn't much better, but at least it's only the one job."

"Why?" he asked. "You're an accountant. What could possibly go wrong?"

"My reputation was trashed after an investigation because people said I was stealing from the company. And, believe me, it's not something I like to talk about."

He snorted. "They obviously didn't know you well." He glanced at her. "Didn't they figure out they were wrong?"

"They did, but it was too late to save my reputation. They said that trust had been broken, and they were sorry, but they had to let me go."

He winced. "Trust on your side for them was broken, I'm sure, but they have no business not trusting you if their allegations were wrong."

"That's what I thought," she said. "But, hey, that was months ago."

"Well, shit, Tanya. It sure does sound like you've had a crappy year."

"Yes," she said. "Now I live in a small apartment by myself and work at a department store, my degree worthless."

"Damn," he said.

"At least you have a job, even if it's tracking down dogs in other countries," she said. "Of course it's not the job you used to do. I'm sorry about that."

"Thanks. It's not as if I'm getting paid for this job," he said quietly. "And I get my navy pension and disability, but it's not the same thing as having a career."

"Ain't that the truth," she said. "I spent years on my career, and now I don't even have that."

"Have you tried applying for other accounting jobs?"

"I have," she said. "Nobody in town will risk hiring me. My reputation precedes me. And I don't have references."

"That sucks and is hardly fair. Particularly if they cleared you of any wrongdoing."

"They did, but it didn't wipe out the bad times getting to that point."

"Why didn't you move? Look elsewhere for a job?"

"I have friends here, people like family. Technically my family is here too."

Lucas tilted his head, raised one eyebrow.

"I may have lost Claire, but I still visit her grave weekly, talk to her. Just like Alice may still be in a coma, but I speak to her too most nights. I hope to be there when she wakes up. I believe she hears me talking to her, that it helps her to heal. As for my biological family," she said, glancing at him, "I'm working through that. Or trying to. And, if and when, maybe I can confront those issues with my mom." She waved both hands, as if dismissing that hard subject. "But I could be much worse off, Lucas. Look at Claire and Alice."

"True. But, counting your job loss, that's three really crappy things in a row," he said. "Sounds like way too big of a coincidence."

"It really does, right? I wasn't sure if I should be suspicious of that. But nothing else has happened to me. Nothing stood out at work that seemed odd. So I don't know what I could have known or seen that I shouldn't have, or what Alice and Claire could have known or seen that they shouldn't have, to warrant all this." Tanya appeared to struggle for a moment before she added, "What happened to you that sent you to the hospital?" she asked.

He paused and took a deep breath before replying. "I was in Iraq, working on a special training mission, and one of the men from the Iraq team, who was a mole, shot six of us. The rest of the US team ended up shooting him and his team. Two of us lived. Four of us died. All of the Iraq team died."

He knew he sounded cold, but it had taken him a while to give any explanation. They had been his friends; they weren't just men. They weren't just some *team*. They were friends—men he had trained with, had worked alongside, had trusted, and they were gone in a heartbeat from something that had no reasonable explanation.

"I'm sorry."

"So am I. They were my friends. The four men who died

all had wives and families."

"Awful," she whispered. "The other guy who survived?"

"He lost both legs," he said quietly. "He's still in rehab, but he's doing much better."

"I'm glad to hear that," she said. "Prosthetics aren't what they used to be."

"That field has come a long way. I worked with a specialist out of New Mexico, and her stuff is cutting-edge." An odd silence followed, and he looked at her and raised an eyebrow. "What?"

"You have prosthetics?"

"My left foot," he said and turned back to face the road. "I can stand without a prosthetic but not for very long. The stump hasn't got enough scar tissue built up for me to put too much pressure on it."

"Oh ..."

"We're a pair, aren't we?" he asked with a half laugh. "Who knew this is where we would end up."

"I often wondered if I deserved this," she said. "Or if it was connected to you because everything happened after I broke up with you."

"Is that why you wanted to come on this drive?" he asked curiously. "To see if I was doing something to cause it?"

"No. *No*, I never blamed you," she exclaimed. "*Never.* I'm the one who broke up with you. Just the thought of learning about fate and karma made me realize how much I still had to let go of and needed to work on."

"Fate? Karma? Aren't those the sister bitches?" he asked with a smile. "We joke about them a lot in the military. Because there is always the sense that another force is out there, keeping us alive when we have a close call or wondering why my four friends ..." he said, swallowing before continuing, "died, and I survived."

"Back to that old saying that karma's a bitch," she said. "If I believed in it, I'd wonder what I could possibly have done so wrong that would have taken my career out as it did. I've never done anything to hurt anyone intentionally," she said. "So why the hell did this all happen to me?"

"I think that's the hardest thing too," he said. "The fact that we never get any answers. You can ask why until you're blue in the face, and you're still left with no answers."

"Is that how you felt after waking up in a hospital room to find your friends were gone?"

"They had to strap me down," he said. "I was determined to go after the son of a bitch who had done that to them. I didn't even listen. I was so mad with pain and anger and grief that it took days for me to calm down. They kept knocking me out with drugs because I kept trying to get out of my hospital bed. I ripped out stitches and caused more damage because I was a stubborn fool, looking for revenge."

"But he was already dead, right?"

"Yes he was, but I had taken that incident into my nightmares; and every time I surfaced, in my brain I was sure I was still caught up in that war and that he was there facing me. It took days before I understood it was really over, and he was dead. I had lost my chance to get revenge. It also took days to assimilate that I had lost four of my best friends."

"I'm so sorry," she said, her voice soft. "I only lost one."

"It doesn't matter if it's one or four," he said. "It hurts like hell."

CHAPTER 3

AFTER THAT HEAVY discussion, they had a mostly lighthearted conversation until they reached their destination. Thankfully it gave her time to adjust to being with him. She was so damn sorry that she hadn't been there for him while he'd been recovering. He shouldn't have gone through that alone.

They each eased out of the truck, took a deep breath and stretched. It felt good to move.

"I haven't done a road trip like that in a long time," she said. "And never in this direction."

He laughed. "This is nothing."

She smiled. "Still, when you are used to driving five minutes to work or five minutes to the grocery store, then four hours in a vehicle? Well, that takes a bit of getting used to."

"Yes, then it does." He walked steadily into the Red Deer Rescue Center, and she followed. He walked with a normal gait, seemingly unaffected by the prosthetic. She wondered what that looked like and felt like. But it was almost unnoticeable, and, if he hadn't told her, she wouldn't have had a clue. Inside the center, he asked for Clarence Jobin.

The woman on the other side of the counter smiled and said, "Clarence isn't here today."

"That's fine," Lucas said. "I'm here to pick up the War Dog Top Hat."

"Oh! You're the one," she said. "I have a message for you." She picked up a piece of paper addressed to him and passed it to him.

He opened the note, scanned it quickly and frowned. "Clarence gave Top Hat to somebody else? Even though he knew I was coming from the US government's War Dogs division?"

The woman looked worried. "Are you actually here on behalf of the US government?"

Lucas drew himself up to his full height. "I specifically said we were here at US Commander Cross's request to track down this dog."

"The dog went nuts," she said hurriedly. "He started attacking everyone. As it happened, we had one of the better dog trainers in the area here, and he said he would take him until you got here."

At that Lucas seemed to relax. "Where is Top Hat? I can pick him up right now."

She pointed to the bottom of the letter. "There's a phone number."

Lucas pulled out his phone and dialed the number. As it rang, he asked the woman before him, "When did he pick up the dog?"

"Two days ago."

Tanya stood beside Lucas as he waited for someone to answer the call.

"Pull up this address please, Tanya," Lucas said, showing her the note. "Find out how far he is from here."

She nodded.

When someone spoke on the other end, Lucas said,

"This is Lucas Scott. I'm here to pick up Top Hat, the shepherd you collected from the rescue center. I believe you're holding him for me."

"Well, that would be nice," the voice said.

The lady behind the counter was close enough to hear that much. Tanya leaned in closer.

Realizing they were trying to listen in, Lucas hit Speaker and placed his phone on the counter so all three could hear. The voice continued, "But he escaped yesterday morning. We've been looking for him since then."

"Shit," Lucas said. "How did he escape?"

"I have six-foot fences not eight-foot fences," the voice on the other end said in exasperation. "He couldn't have gone too far, but I don't want to take any chances, as he was very aggressive at the center, and we don't want him to attack anyone."

"He's a trained military dog," Lucas said. "He understands commands very well."

"He wasn't listening to any commands I gave him," the man snapped. "You are welcome to help us hunt for him."

"We'll be there in twenty minutes," Lucas said. He ended the call, put away his phone and glared at the woman on the other side of the counter. "There will be repercussions for this." He snatched up the note and walked out.

Hating to see the worried look on the woman's face, Tanya said, "It's really important that we find that dog."

The woman nodded. "We just couldn't keep him here," she said. "It was a godsend Andy was here as it was because we had no other place for the dog."

"Andy who? And you couldn't have just separated Top Hat from other dogs? Or brought a vet in to tranquilize him?"

"Andy Ross." The woman looked even more worried. "I don't know. I don't make those decisions, and I wasn't here at the time," she offered hurriedly. "I'm sorry. I hope you find him."

"You better hope we do," Tanya said. "This was an official request. He's come a long way to get this dog."

The woman nodded and watched until she left.

Tanya hurried outside and jumped in the truck. "It looked like you were about to take off without me."

"Only if I have to," he said and turned out of the parking lot, spitting gravel behind.

"Is it that bad?"

"If the dog is put down, yes," he said.

"If the dog is aggressive, maybe he needs to be put down." And she realized she had said the wrong thing because the look he gave her was black and dark. "Why do you care so much?" she asked.

"Because I'd been on missions where those dogs saved our asses," he said. "And a dog saved my life this last time too."

"Seriously?"

He nodded. "That dog gave his life and took the bullets intended for me," he said. "If there is *anything* I can do to help this dog, I will. We train them. We put them through hell, and then, when they finally get a chance to have a bit of a life, something like this happens. It takes a special person to deal with them."

"But are you that person?" she asked.

"I worked with them over there, although I wasn't a handler or a trainer. I was on a team with two dogs. You get used to working with them, and they followed orders incredibly well."

"Still …" she said, "you need a place to keep a dog like that."

"Nathan's got kennels," he said. "We have to capture Top Hat, get him checked out so I can get him across the border, but, after that, I'm not sure what'll happen to him."

"Are you looking to maybe keep him long-term?"

"I'm not sure," he replied and shrugged. "You're asking questions I don't have answers for."

She realized there wasn't anything to be gained by pushing him. She was worried about a dog that aggressive. One that could escape six-foot fences. She hoped they would have a good ending to this.

He turned to look at her and asked, "Did you have plans you need to be back for?"

She shook her head. "No. I don't work until day after tomorrow. So, if we are delayed today, it's fine."

"Good," he said. "Because obviously this trip will not be as quick as I thought it would be." He let out a slow breath.

She realized he must have been stressed about getting her back home today. Tanya let out a slow breath as well and smiled. She was relieved they would be spending more time together. Nothing waited for her back home. And all she wanted was sitting right beside her.

HE DROVE TO the address with his truck's GPS spitting out instructions every step of the way. When he reached his destination, he parked his truck and hopped out. From where he stood in front of the house, he could see what appeared to be a good five acres, fenced and cross-fenced.

That made him feel a bit better.

He had been worried somebody hadn't taken care of the dog, so the dog had been desperate to get free. But that didn't look to be the way of it. At least the property was clean, well-cared-for, and the fences were strong. He rang the doorbell, and the door was opened immediately.

"Hi, I'm Andy. You must be Lucas."

Lucas nodded and said, "I am. Can you show me where Top Hat disappeared from?"

Andy shrugged and said, "I do this all the time. We pick up a lot of dogs the shelter can't handle. I work to rehabilitate them and then find them homes, but this shepherd wouldn't be kept in by anybody."

"That's possible," Lucas said. "The history on the dog since he left the military has been sketchy. I'm not sure what happened or how he ended up in the rescue pack coming up here because the tattoo should easily have been tracked back to the War Dogs department."

"I don't know anything about that," Andy said with alarm. "The shelter called me in a panic and said they had a dog they had a problem with and couldn't get a vet to come in and deal with. They didn't have anybody there capable of taking care of him since just the support staff was on duty. So I went in and managed to get him tied up and crated. I put him out here in one of my pens, and, next thing I know, he was gone."

Andy led the way through the house out to the back. Lucas checked once to make sure Tanya was with him. She kept very close to his side. As they walked outside, they were greeted by barking dogs. Four of the dogs were milling around, happy-go-lucky and obviously at ease with strangers.

Andy led them over to a pen at the back. "He was in here. As you can see, he's no longer here."

It was, indeed, a strong wire pen, basically a deer fence, with square holes through it and six feet high with solid steel posts.

Lucas stared at the pen and shook his head. "Bud, no offense, but that is the worst fencing for keeping a dog in." He knew his tone was abrupt, but he was not impressed.

Andy looked at him in surprise. "And why is that?" he asked.

"Because dogs can climb. That fencing is stiff and firm, and, once they can get their paws and toes hooked in, it gives them strong support, and they can get up and over."

Tanya snorted a laugh behind him before abruptly quieting.

Lucas looked at Andy. "Same issue with using logs of wood. Anything they can get a grip on."

Andy nodded. "I've never had anyone escape before. So it's never been an issue."

"This is a War Dog. He can get in and out of places he needed to get in and out of quietly. It was all part of his training. He can also scale eight-foot fences, but, of course, he didn't come with a warning sign, did he? Other than that War Dogs tattoo, right?" Lucas let out a short laugh, realizing his tone might have been brusque. It was a tense situation. He had come all this way to find the dog had taken himself out of the picture.

"I'm sorry," Andy said. "What do you want to do?"

"I'll find him," Lucas replied. "Anything else is not an option."

"There's another problem," Andy said. "An underground dogfighting group is here in town. Well, across several towns in fact."

"Right. That would be a problem. What are the options?"

"The dog is either wild and fends for himself and eventually he will return, or he'll try to find somewhere he is comfortable, but I doubt that will be the shelter or here," Andy said. "Or he'll get picked up by someone else, and, if it is someone from the dogfighting group, that's bad news."

"I know the cops have taken down two large dogfighting rings," Tanya said, "but that was a couple hours from here."

"The ring is pretty widespread and always hunting for new dogs," Andy said. "If you took down two, that's good, but there's probably at least two more. A lot of local families are involved in that sport. A big male like Top Hat, well, he'll be prime dogfighting material."

"That's so cruel," Tanya said.

"Yes, it is," Andy said. "Especially when you get dogs that don't want to fight. It's an ugly sport with a lot of ugly people involved, and that's something we're all doing the best we can to try to stop it."

"What if we checked out those places first?" Lucas asked, his arms over his chest. "I've got no objection to going in and letting those dogs loose."

"You can't just let them loose," Andy protested. "They need a lot of medical attention. And the aggressive ones don't know how to calm down anymore. They've been trained for this, and they don't know anything different."

"Is anybody working to solve this? Here at least?" Lucas asked. "Ones who I could connect with and maybe could help out?"

"Sure," Andy said, nodding. "If you think that's what you want to do, you take that step. Though you can get in more trouble than you are expecting. These people are very protective. This is against the law, so it'll land them in jail,

40

and they could lose their homes. That makes them very dangerous. They have a lot to lose."

"Good," Lucas said. "Every home lost is another one they can't use to train more animals for fighting."

"I hear you," Andy said. "It's not that easy though. You know that, right?"

"It never is," Lucas said. "But the fact of the matter is, if we don't do *something,* nothing gets done."

"Agreed," Andy said. "I might have someone I can call. Hang on a moment." He disappeared inside only to return dialing his cellphone. But it seemed to ring and just ring. "Sorry I can't get a hold of him, I'll try again later."

"Not a problem," Lucas said. "I'll be fine."

Tanya stepped closer and asked, "Are you sure you want to get into this?"

"I *do*," Lucas said affirmatively. He looked at her and smiled. "Have you ever known me not to go after the underdog and find a cause to fight for?"

"Sure, but remember what I said about Claire?"

"Yes, and that's an even better reason," he said. "We're only four hours apart here. There's nothing good about dogfighting. So if we can't stop it here, we can probably stop it there. But I don't want to sit here and pick up one or two people involved in abusing dogs by setting up these dog-fighting rings. I want to take them all out."

She winced. "It's great to be ambitious. but you could pick something that's not quite so dangerous," she said on a laugh.

He half smirked. "Not likely to happen. Remember the work I used to do? To protect the innocent? This time I am not traveling overseas and not working for the navy, but I sure as hell am not ready to give up helping out others.

Particularly War Dogs and other dogs being abused."

"It's dangerous," she said as she worried her bottom lip.

"It is," he said. "But it is much more dangerous for the dogs. I'm more than happy to just retrieve Top Hat, but, if he has been taken into a dogfighting ring, he's in trouble. Top Hat deserves a home where he doesn't have to fight and doesn't have to listen to explosions and doesn't have to go to war each and every day."

"How do you get him to stay? A six-foot fence wasn't enough to keep him contained. What is?"

"Easy," he said with a big smile. "You don't force the dog to stay. You make it so he wants to stay. So that it is his choice because that's where he wants to be. You can't ever hold a rebel in. You can curtail their freedom and keep an eye on them and punish them every time, but the only real way to get them to stay is to win their loyalty and to make them want to stay. It sounds impossible. I know. But it works."

"No," she said quietly. "It sounds about right because it's the same for men, isn't it? Or any relationship. It's about loyalty, respect, wanting to be where they are. And not feeling hemmed in and penned in, like a prisoner."

He looked at her in surprise. "Well, that was never a problem with us."

She smiled. "No," she said. "I could always trust you, and I could always count on you."

He nodded. "That's just who I am, and I won't let these dogs down any more than I would let you down."

She looked at him for a long moment and nodded. "Very true. You didn't let me down. I'm the one who let you down." She took a deep breath and looked him in the eyes. "For that, I am very sorry."

He stared at her in shock. "What brought this on?"

She gave him a sad smile. "A realignment of values," she said, "and finally realizing what truly matters."

CHAPTER 4

S HE HADN'T EXPECTED to get into this conversation like this, but no doubt it was one that needed to happen. She was also disturbed by the look of complete shock on his face. She shrugged and turned to look at Andy, now rejoining them. "Sorry. Personal business."

Andy's gaze went from one to the other, interest lighting up his face. "Nothing like star-crossed lovers," he said. "Keeps life interesting. At least for those of us on the outside."

"Not too interesting for me," Lucas said drily. "More like tormenting. Any idea where those involved in this lovely dogfighting ring live?"

"Not really," Andy said. "I've worked with some cops to help bring down a couple. I usually go in when they do the raids to help collect some of the dogs. Often the dogs are so traumatized we have to put them down." He shook his head and stared off in the distance. "Sometimes I hate people. I have an idea where a couple are, but you can't just go in there without any backup."

Lucas shoved his hands in his pockets and studied Andy. "Can you tell me the names of who you work with within the police department?"

Andy nodded. "I can do that."

"Also do you have any idea where my dog might have

gone to?" he asked.

Andy shook his head. "Out there," he said. His arm spread out toward the wide-open country around them. "I have to assume the dog got out on his own because all the gates are still locked."

"That was my next question," Lucas said. "Whether somebody might have stolen him."

"The dog wasn't very friendly," Andy said, his tone dry. "Honestly, even if somebody did want him for dogfighting, they'd have to manhandle him first."

Lucas nodded. "Not a nice thought either. The dog won't be cooperative."

"No, he isn't." At that Andy led the way back to the house. They stopped in the kitchen where he pulled out a notebook. He opened and flipped through several pages and then ripped a piece out of the back and started writing down some names. "These are the two cops I've dealt with. Talk to them. They'll keep an eye out for Top Hat, and, if you have any pictures of the dog, it could help maybe locate him. I don't have any myself. Didn't have him long enough."

"Good enough," Lucas said. "You can expect to see me back here tomorrow. I'll take Tanya home, but I'll return and track Top Hat from here."

"If you're going to track him, you should start now," Andy said. "The weather is turning tonight."

Lucas winced. "Rain?"

"Yes. And lots of it."

Lucas stared out the window.

Tanya realized she'd become a problem. "Go do what you gotta do," she said. "I'm fine. I can wait in the truck."

"You don't have to wait in the truck," Andy said. "I doubt tracking the dog will do you any good, but you might as well do it and leave her in the comfort of my home. I don't mind if she hangs out. I've got work to do with the animals for the next hour anyway." He glanced at her and smiled. "Make yourself at home."

She could see Lucas hesitating. She urged him on. "Go. Go. Go. Time's a wasting."

He nodded and slipped out the front door. She watched him leave, Andy at her side, as Lucas went to the same place in the fence they had assumed Top Hat had gone over and watched as he glared at the ground for a bit, then bolted in one direction, which was not the direction she would have guessed.

"Does he know what he's doing?" Andy asked.

"That's the one thing about Lucas you can be sure of. He always knows what he's doing," she muttered. Then she plastered a bright smile on her face. "He's ex-military. He tracks like crazy."

"Oh, well, in that case ..." Andy said with a nod. "Maybe he'll have some luck then." He turned to her. "Help yourself to tea or coffee if you want, but I have to get back out and start working."

She waved him off. "I appreciate the hospitality," she said. "I have my phone with me. It'll keep me busy."

He nodded and disappeared out the back.

As soon as he was gone, the thought of tea appealed. She wondered if she should take his generosity to heart. She glanced around the kitchen and spotted a kettle. She grabbed it and filled it with water to boil. Various boxes of tea sat on the counter; she chose the herbal tea and found a clean mug.

Once it was ready, she sat in the living room and relaxed. She wondered if it would be hours before Lucas returned. Her phone rang. It was Meg. She smiled as she answered. "Hey. We're at a guy's house who was supposed to keep Top Hat for a couple days and help calm him down, but the dog jumped over a six-foot fence and disappeared into the wild. Lucas has gone after him."

Meg sighed. "Of course he has," she said. "So you guys won't be home anytime soon, will you?"

"No," Tanya said. "We haven't even left yet."

"Okay. I won't worry about you for dinner then," she said in a cheerful voice. "How's it going between the two of you?"

"Better than expected," Tanya replied. "I was telling him about Alice and Claire. I'm happy to not be in town myself. I would have just spent it at Alice's bedside."

"I know," Meg said, her voice dropping in sympathy. "I'm sure Lucas had no idea what had happened to your friends."

"No," Tanya said, staring out at the yard. "He did bring up something though. ... He thought they might be connected."

"What do you mean?" Meg asked, her voice sharp.

"I never thought I would find myself here, dealing with another dogfighting ring. But that's apparently one of the dangers to animals at shelters like this. It's one of the reasons why Lucas was so adamant about tracking down the dog, to make sure he doesn't end up in a dogfighting ring."

"And that has what to do with your girlfriends?"

"Claire was mauled by a dog allegedly. I don't know all the details though."

"That's got nothing to do with what happened to Alice though, does it?"

"I don't know. Yet," Tanya said.

"You were almost always with them, Tanya. That means

you could be in danger too."

"It's possible," Tanya replied.

"The sooner you guys get back here, the better," Meg said, her voice suddenly nervous. "Are you okay?"

"We are okay," Tanya said. "We're talking at least. But nothing too personal."

"As long as you're clearing the air, getting it all out. You might end up with a friendship out of this."

"I want more than a friendship," Tanya said boldly, knowing that was not what Meg expected.

Meg sounded startled, and then she finally said, "Are you sure? He was really hurt last time. I'm not sure he's up for more. Hell, I'm not sure I'm up for him going through more. Before you go down that path, you have to be damn sure you know where you want to go."

"I want to go the same damn place I always wanted to go," Tanya said. "I am still not sure about some of it, but I really don't want to lose Lucas."

"Losing Lucas is one thing. Kicking Lucas away again, now that's a separate thing entirely," Meg warned, her voice protective, edgy even. "Don't do this to him again." And she ended the call.

Tanya immediately called her friend back. "Meg, please. I don't want to lose you or Lucas. And I especially don't want to cause him any more grief or pain. He's been through enough."

"That's for sure," Meg snapped.

"Look, Meg. I understand you want to protect Lucas. I want to protect him too. He and I are talking things out. And, after losing Claire, and Alice too in a different sense, I really appreciate the friends I do have. The healthy ones. Like you, Meg. So just remember that I love you. And I love

Lucas. Always have. And I have issues"—she laughed at the benign word—"that I need to work out fully. Or at least more than I have to date."

Meg lightly chuckled.

"So Lucas coming here brought this all to a head. It's time. It's high time he and I fixed our issues." Tanya quieted, could hear Meg breathing softly on the other end. "I want this to work out right for all of us this time."

"Me too," Meg said. "With all of us happy."

"Exactly."

HE COULD SEE Top Hat's tracks where he'd landed on the other side of the fence, his paws digging into the soft dirt, and then a few leaps as he had dug in and raced away as fast as he could. At least it gave Lucas a direction. He took off following the tracks, trying hard to keep an eye on where he was going. It was easy to get turned around and to lose sight of the landmarks. He'd been tracking for many years and instinctively kept note of north and south, so he could come back to his point of origin.

Running up a hill with a prosthetic was not an easy job. By the time he reached the top, he swore at himself for it. The tracks kept going downhill. He picked up the pace, even though the dog was a good day ahead, knowing the dog could have ended up finding a place and just sticking close by. Lucas could see farms and other properties at the bottom of the hill and wouldn't be at all surprised if the dog had taken to resting somewhere out of sight at one of them.

If there was a barn, he'd have taken that himself. As he approached the properties, he saw a man working. He called out to him. When the guy walked over, Lucas asked if he had seen a dog.

The man shook his head and said, "Nope. But, during the night, I heard a bit of a ruckus. By the time I came outside, I saw no sign of anyone." He glanced around. "I don't have chickens anymore. Otherwise, I suspect at least one would have been dead by now."

Lucas nodded. "In this case, the dog's desperate. He's lost. He's a military dog, but he's difficult to handle. I came to pick him up, but the rescue center that had him let him go to a trainer, and the trainer lost him."

"Andy?"

"Yeah, at Andy's place."

"He's been known to deal with a lot of difficult dogs."

"But I'm getting the impression you don't mean that in a nice way."

"Let's just say, I've had my suspicions about him. Don't trust him. Maybe he's turned over a new leaf. I don't know."

"What would his old leaf have been like?" Lucas asked, wanting to know more. Something about this whole setup was off. "Was he involved in dogfighting?"

The farmer nodded. "He was charged too. This was a long time ago, but I guess, from my point of view, you're either an animal lover or you're not. And if you are, you don't put dogs into fights."

"Right. How long ago was this. Do you know?"

"Ten years maybe? To be honest, for all I know, he's completely turned over a new leaf and dedicated his life to protecting dogs. That's certainly the line he feeds everybody, but I don't know that I believe it."

"Fair enough," Lucas said. He handed over his card. "If you do catch sight of the dog, don't approach him. Just call me, please."

The farmer nodded. "Is that his picture on here?"

"No," he said. "That's one of my old dogs."

The farmer smiled.

"I worked with a lot of K9s in the military. So I was delegated to come get him and take him home."

"It sounds like you're the right man to do this then." The farmer waved and headed back to work.

Lucas headed to the next property and the next. He could see Top Hat's tracks had slowed, and there were even several places where he lay down. He needed water, and he needed food. Lucas found a spot where the dog could go under one of the fences to a nearby watering hole for horses—a great big barrel with an automatic drip line attached. He could see the dog tracks up to the water and knew Top Hat had tanked up pretty well at that point.

But he was still a good twelve hours ahead of him and that could mean anything. Lucas kept walking to the next property and saw Top Hat's tracks once again. The dog was limping now. But then he had had a hard run and was now very tired. Lucas kept tracking until he got to a creek. He stopped there. If Top Hat had walked down to the water, which he might have with a sore paw, it was hard to see where he would have come out on the other side.

Did he have a reason to cross the river? Well, if he had been chased, he would certainly do so, and a dog's whim to carry on going north was rarely sidelined by water. He would have also taken the opportunity to have tanked up even more. Lucas crossed the river himself, using rocks to stay mostly above the water line. When he got to the other side, he searched the banks, looking for where the dog might have come out.

He was only up about twenty to thirty feet when saw it. The dog had come out on the side Lucas was on and had walked along a trail. Frowning, Lucas kept going, then realized this was becoming quite a trip. It was all one way so far. Away from Tanya. He picked up his phone and dialed her.

"Where are you?" she asked.

"About an hour's run, up the hill, down the other side, and about ten properties away. The dog's still heading down the creek path."

"Interesting," she said.

"How are you feeling there?" he asked, wondering how much he should tell her. Then he decided, if there was any chance the information he'd gotten was true, then she could be in danger. "I heard some disturbing news that maybe Andy isn't as innocent in all of this as he led us to believe."

He heard her small gasp. "What do you mean?"

"Apparently he was charged with dogfighting a decade ago and had a place potentially for breeding. Now maybe he's turned a new leaf and is looking to protect dogs, but I'm not so sure. The man who shared the information didn't seem to think so either."

"Okay. That's *not* good," she said. "Why don't I hop in the truck and drive down to where you are? Because I don't like the sound of what you're telling me."

"I'm not telling you anything except that potentially Andy might not be as innocent as he said."

"I'm already outside the house now," she said. "Please tell me you left the keys in the truck."

"A spare set's above the visor," he said. He heard his truck door open and her hop in. "Did you find them?"

"Yeah, I did," she said through the phone. The engine

53

turned over, and the gear shift changed.

"Good thing you know how to drive a truck," he said with a bit of laughter in his tone.

"I'd be driving this sucker even if I didn't know how," she said. "Because anybody who'll raise dogs to fight each other is not anybody I want to hang around with. Especially alone."

"I'm more concerned about what he'll do to keep his business quiet," Lucas said seriously. "When you hit the bottom of that driveway turn right and go down the hill, then take a right. Look for some sort of open space, like a public park with a parking lot. I'm at the corner of that."

"I'll be there soon," she said and ended the call.

He walked to the parking lot. What he needed to know was whether Top Hat kept going or whether he'd been picked up by someone or was hiding. He stopped when he got to the far end of the parking lot and swore.

There was a red stain on the ground. In his mind, he knew what had happened. Somebody had shot the damn dog. It didn't mean that Top Hat was dead; it could have been just a graze or a tranq to subdue the aggressive dog. But it wasn't good either way.

He pulled out his phone and looked up the numbers Andy had given him. He called the first one, and, when Detective Madison answered, Lucas identified who he was and what he was doing. "Any chance you can check to see if an aggressive dog was dispatched or if you had any incident involving one. I'm at ..." He turned to look around. "I think it's called Cedar Creek Park," he said.

"I don't have any report on file," the detective said. "This dog's military trained, did you say?"

"Yes," Lucas replied. "It could be somebody tried to stop

him, and he didn't want to get stopped."

"I don't know if Andy told you, but we've got quite a problem here with people kidnapping aggressive dogs or big dogs and putting them in fights."

"I heard something about that. I am also a little concerned that apparently Andy has a record for dogfighting himself."

There was a long span of silence on the other end. "I'm not sure I heard that before," the detective said, his voice flat. "I think I'll have to look into it."

"You do that," Lucas said. "I'm not trying to cause trouble for anyone, and I'm certainly not in a position to know Andy, but one of the neighbors I stopped to ask if he'd seen Top Hat warned me about Andy's history."

"Interesting," the detective said, his voice harsher than it had been. "We'll keep an eye out for the dog. If you've seen blood, chances are he might have been taken."

"That's not good news," Lucas said, swearing, "because it could just as easily have been Andy."

"But you've got no reason to think that, do you?"

"No," he said. "Not really. At least not without more proof. He seemed friendly and helpful, but I don't know how much of that was part of his cover. He gave me a couple areas in town known to have dogfights and for breeding in the past."

"Yeah, we've got two bad areas in town." The detective told him the locations.

Lucas looked at the paper. "Yes, that's the areas Andy gave me. Maybe I'll do a drive-by and see if I come up with anything."

"What's that dog doing up here anyway?" the detective asked.

"Somehow he was mixed in with a group of rescue dogs coming across the border," Lucas said. "But he's definitely not one that should have been brought in. Uncle Sam's already trying to figure out what happened to him but there are no clear answers."

"Are you taking him back when you do find him?"

"My job is to find him and to make sure he's okay, and, in this instance, he's obviously not," Lucas said, looking around and seeing his truck coming down the road. He waved at Tanya. "If he were to be in a decent home, then we'd be fine with it. But, at the moment, obviously we can't leave him where he is."

"No," the detective agreed. "Because if anybody has him for fighting, we'll end up with a whole pile of dead dogs."

"Which is why I'm really concerned," Lucas said. "Talk about a disadvantage for any other dogs in the pen. None of it is good news."

"No, it's not," the detective cut in. "Keep in touch, will you? I don't want to think you're running off and getting into trouble. We don't want to find somebody else dead in this game."

"What do you mean, *somebody else*?"

"A young woman was killed not long ago, not in town here but a few hours away. She was one of our dispatchers. There's a suspicion her death was linked to the dogfighting world."

"Claire Lamont," Lucas said, his voice harsh. "She was the best friend of my ex. Actually Tanya is here with me now."

"Well, let's hope nobody sees her," the detective said. "Because we're hearing from the underground that they killed one, potentially attacked another and possibly looking for the third."

Just then Tanya pulled up, shut off the engine and hopped out.

Lucas watched her, his heart sinking as he realized he might've dragged her somewhere that was the worst place for her to be. "How serious do you think that rumor is?" he asked the detective. He reached out a hand, gratified when Tanya placed hers in his. "Because Tanya is here with me. I don't want her in any danger."

The cop hesitated. "I'd like to tell you to go right back home, but you came here on a mission. There is nothing I can say that will slow you down or stop you, is there?"

"No," Lucas said. "But I can take Tanya back and keep her out of trouble."

"You might want to keep her with you. That way you can make sure she stays safe."

"Nobody warned her to be careful. Why not?" Lucas demanded. "If you had any suspicion, she should have been warned."

"This tip just came in yesterday," he said. "We passed the information on to the station closest to her last night. Chances are good they are trying to contact her right now."

"I'll talk to her about it," he said. "Thanks for the heads-up."

"You take care." The detective ended the call.

Lucas watched Tanya as he slowly pocketed his phone. His face was serious as he asked her, "Have you had any phone calls from the cops today?"

She pulled out her phone. "I missed two calls. They were the same number, but I didn't call back. Figured I'd do that when we got home." She frowned as she looked at the number. "I don't recognize it."

"Cops. Apparently they've gotten wind of some rumors that Claire's and Alice's cases might have been connected. The people involved with that also might be looking for their roommate." He watched as the color drained from Tanya's face.

She reached out her free hand and placed it on the hood of the truck for support. "Seriously?"

He nodded grimly. "In other words, you're in danger now."

She gave a bitter laugh. "Both of my friends were attacked in my hometown. We're almost four hours away. Still in dogfighting country regardless. What difference does it make?"

He had to give her that. "True enough," he said. "I am tracking down a loose dog that may or may not have been shot and taken." He pointed to the cement so she could see the red patch.

She shook her head. "Surely somebody didn't just shoot the dog and then throw him in the garbage, did they?"

"Or they shot him to wound him, and they'll keep him for fighting. Once he's healed, into the ring he'll go."

She stared at him. "Why are people such assholes?" she cried out. "That dog is innocent."

"He won't be soon," Lucas said. "Once he starts fighting and killing, he'll have a hard time walking back from that."

"We have to find him," she said. "And we have to find him now."

He smiled. "That's why I'm here. But—"

"No. I'm not going anywhere. I know you think I would be safe away from you, but I think the safest place for me is wherever you are. They might get me if I'm alone, but they won't try anything when you are around."

"No," he agreed. "They won't. I won't let them."

"Exactly," she said, her voice faint. "Believe me. I never doubted that you cared all these years, and I always knew you'd do your best to keep me safe. But none of us could have expected this."

He nodded. "None of us could have expected this."

CHAPTER 5

TANYA HADN'T EXPECTED to have her life play out this way, but the added news that she could be hunted down by the very same people who had killed Claire and had almost killed Alice was not something that sat well. She knew her best chance at staying alive was to remain with Lucas. Her friends had been taken out fast and expertly. She didn't know if losing her job was part of this or just shitty timing, but she'd had enough rough times. She wouldn't put it past these people, but why would they bother? Easier to just kill her outright.

"Keep me with you," she whispered. "It's not how I wanted us to come together, and I certainly don't want you to feel like you have to look after me. But I also know, if somebody is hunting me, I'm as good as dead." She shook her head, tears filling her eyes. She brushed them away impatiently. "Both of my friends? That's just too unbelievable."

"The good news is, the cops know. They are on it."

"It's been my biggest fear since Alice and Claire. I mean, obviously with one dead and one in the hospital, I had to consider maybe I was next. I pushed it off as being too far a reach. And if it isn't too far out there, then I wish I knew how or why. It makes no sense."

"You know something you don't know that you know."

Lucas shrugged. "And, if you happen to be seen with me here, it could put you in more danger or keep you safer. Who knows how these people think?"

Her breath released in a raspy gasp. "I won't be treated as collateral damage, not if you're here," she said. And she definitely didn't want to be separated from him. She reached up a shaky hand, noting just how unnerved she really was, and then gave a broken laugh. "Wow, how to absolutely ruin my life."

"I'm sorry," he said abruptly. "Maybe I shouldn't have told you."

She shot him a hard look. "No. I'm glad you told me. Better to know and do what I can to stay safe than be blindsided. So now what?"

"I'll head to the area where the dogfighting is, but I can't have you with me."

"In case I'm recognized?"

"Because I won't be just looking for those involved. If there is a dogfight going on, I'm going in."

"You can't do it alone. You need backup. Men trained for this."

He pulled out his phone. "I just talked to a detective. I'm pretty sure I can get some help if it looks like a dogfight is in the works. Or if I see an arena and dogs in kennels."

"It's still dangerous as hell," she said.

"It is," he said. "Doesn't mean I don't do it just because it's dangerous. I'm still doing what's right."

She pinched her lips together and glared at him. Why did he have to play the hero? "One person is already dead. Another lying in a coma. You could be next. I can't live with that."

He smiled. "That part of my life hasn't changed."

She stared off in the distance, realizing he was right. It was one of the things she'd always had trouble with. The fact that he'd go into a dangerous line of work, and she was supposed to just wait for him to come home. Actually it wasn't the waiting part as much as the not-knowing part. She worried about him constantly.

What if he didn't come home?

"You're no longer active military," she said. "Life shouldn't be dangerous for you now."

"When you go to save the underdog, to help, you will encounter those who would oppress you."

"Doesn't have to be you though," she blurted out.

"It doesn't have to be me, but *I* won't be *me* if I don't go. Let's go scope out the area." He walked over to the truck and hopped in. He waited while she got in on her side, and, as she closed the door, he looked at her. "You don't need to stay here. You know that, right?"

"I don't need to stay here for your sake," she said. "I need to stay here for my sake."

He frowned, started the engine and pulled the truck away.

"What will you do if you find out they've shot Top Hat?" She watched a muscle in his jaw twitch. When he didn't answer, she said, "You know you can't kill them."

"I know," he said calmly. "It doesn't mean the dog doesn't get his chance for revenge though. If he's still alive."

LUCAS SHOULDN'T HAVE said that, but it was hard to see these kinds of men get away with the abuses they inflicted. Dogfighting was deadly for the animals, terrorizing for the innocents taken off the street and tossed into a ring with dogs trying to kill them. And for the dog trying to kill them too because he knows it's either kill or be killed. But, with each successive fight, he's got the upper hand because he's already won the last one.

The fact that the local authorities had taken out two dogfighting rings but hadn't gotten the rest meant the others would be that much harder to find. He knew in his heart that was where Top Hat was, and he didn't want that for Top Hat. He hadn't been trained to kill for fun; he killed for survival and would make mincemeat out of an opponent. Then he'd be down a path that would be hard to come back from, which was hardly fair. The dog had given a lot of years to the military; he deserved to retire in peace.

Lucas opened up the glove box and pulled out a map, then tossed it on her lap. "See if you can find the two areas we're looking for."

She unfolded the map and studied the area. Lucas took a right, heading toward town. He'd taken a glance at the map earlier, but that was only enough to get him through town. He didn't know where the rest of the areas were.

"The first is up on the other side of the river."

He picked up speed, merged into traffic and waited for her to chime in with more information.

"They're beside each other," she said thoughtfully. "More rural than we've seen so far with large properties. I'm not sure, but I think one is probably more of a lower-income area. Although, with the rise of the properties' values, it's hard to know. But they are likely hobby farms, not elegant estates."

"Why is that?"

"Because I remember, when that local mill shut down, a

lot of people were out of work. There'd also been a lot of protests and a lot of people complaining about how difficult their lives were."

"I can see that then. Dogfighting is all about betting and trying to make your money somehow."

"Sure, but you've got to have the money to bet it," she said.

"That's all right," he said. "We'll figure it out. We need to get into that area, drive around, scout out the lay of the land, and then we'll find somewhere to stop for a meal."

"Good," she said, "I had a cup of tea at Andy's but that's all."

"Andy. I forgot about him," Lucas said as he turned to look at her. "I'm a little worried he might have been the one who shot Top Hat."

"Then maybe we should be staying around and seeing what he does," she said.

"I thought of it. I'll check this area first because we can't have all our eggs in one basket."

"No," she said. "But, at the moment, we don't have anything."

"Maybe not," he said. "But, once we shake loose a few skeletons, you'll be surprised at how the others come out of the woodwork."

"Which is why I think we could have given Andy the first shakedown," she said.

"When he went out back, do you know where he went?"

"No," she said. "I never saw him again. ... His vehicle was gone when I left though," she said, frowning.

"And you didn't notice him leave, did you?"

She sat back and thought about it, then shook her head. "No, I didn't. How could he have left without me hearing that?"

"He could have rolled it until he got far enough down the driveway to start the engine."

"It was facing down the hill, wasn't it?"

"It certainly was," Lucas said. "I've got the license plate number in my head, and I know the model, and I sure would like to find out where he's gone."

"You really think he's gone after Top Hat?"

"I think he's gone after whoever is holding Top Hat. It is also possible Top Hat is still at his place. We don't know yet."

"Do you really think he's involved?"

"I think it's just too damn convenient that a dog like Top Hat comes to his property, escapes and then gets shot."

"Do you think Top Hat escaped, or did they let him out?"

"I think Top Hat got wind of something very wrong, and he took the opportunity when he could and bolted."

"And that's why they shot him? Because there was no way to bring him in without it?"

"I imagine that was the easiest way to deal with him. I doubt they killed him. I really think, if Top Hat is badly hurt, they'll probably just shoot him, or for training, and, if he's not badly hurt, they'll use him for fighting. And, if he bites one of them, they'll put him in the ring injured and hope the other dog takes him apart."

CHAPTER 6

THEY DROVE THROUGH the streets with purpose as Lucas appeared to know what he was doing, whereas she didn't. All the buildings looked the same. But it was definitely much more of a rural area with lots of barns and horse stables. She glanced from one to the other. "How can you possibly tell where the dogs are?"

"That's the thing. You're not supposed to," he said, "because they don't want anybody knowing. Especially now that those first two rings were brought down."

"But they still need people to come for the fights, right?"

"Right. So, a big-enough location, parking away from the streets, all of that's important."

They drove around for a good hour, and then Lucas pulled into an empty parking spot near a coffee shop. As they walked closer, they noticed several large groups of men in the parking lot.

She motioned at them. He nodded. "Don't worry about it," he said.

"They look like trouble," she said.

He chuckled. "Just because they're in plaid jackets, some wearing jeans, does not mean they are trouble."

"You're not listening," she said. "My instinct says run."

At that, he looked at her. "Seriously?"

She nodded—her shoulders hunched forward. "But

maybe that's because I know I'm being hunted …"

He nodded as he rubbed her back, pushing her closer to the coffee shop. "Our purpose is a little different here. Keep that in mind too."

"Got it," she said. "It's still a little disconcerting."

"Yes, it is," he replied through the side of his mouth. "At least this way everyone sees you are not alone."

She gave a quiet chuckle. "How sad that this is what we have to do to stay safe."

"Not every female is being hunted right now," he said cheerfully.

They stepped through the front doors. The restaurant had two sides of seating. Lucas gave a casual glance around, noting the rest of the patrons, and his back stiffened ever-so-slightly. "We'll sit on the other side," he said calmly, acting as if nothing was different.

But something definitely was, she just didn't know what. She followed him to the other side, and they sat in a corner by the window with the door just a few feet from them.

He walked over to the counter, ordered two coffees, two muffins, paid and brought everything back to the table. As soon as he sat down, she whispered, "What did you see?"

"Andy," he replied in a low tone. He glanced around the street parking and then motioned at a truck parked under the trees. "That's his truck over there."

"Shit," she said. "You think that's why he's here?"

"Oh, I'm pretty sure," he said. "What I need is a picture of the other guys he's with."

"I might be able to do that," Tanya said. "The washroom is on the other side." She subtly pointed to the sign.

"No, not alone," he said.

She snorted. "Hey, I'm here, and it's a washroom.

They're not likely to do anything in the restaurant. Besides, I have to walk by them to go."

Just as she spoke, a woman stood at the next table and said something to the woman still seated there.

"I'll ask her if she knows where the ladies' room is." Pulling out her phone, she put it on Video to record the men for Lucas, then walked up to the woman standing in the aisle. "Excuse me. Do you know where the washroom is?"

The woman smiled, turned and said, "Just follow me. I'm heading there now."

Tanya held out her cell phone, angled in such a way to still be unobtrusive against her as she walked to the washroom, talking to the woman, completely ignoring the men sitting around. She was aware enough to realize Andy was here, but he sank in his chair, as if he realized who she was too.

In the washroom, Tanya used the facilities and walked back out. She kept her phone on Video so she could tape the sitting men. She'd only been able to tape their backs before. When she rejoined Lucas, she said, "Andy was trying to hide." She noted the relief on Lucas's face when she sat down again.

"Of course he is," Lucas said. "Not that he has any reason to yet."

She nodded and handed him her phone. He studied the faces and nodded. "Can you email that to me, please?" He returned her phone to her.

She did as he requested.

The beep marked the receipt of her emailed video. "I'll send this to Badger, a friend of mine, to see if he can run it through their databases." He frowned. "I should also send this to the detective I spoke with but don't have his email address." While she watched, he dialed a number. When a voice answered, he put the phone on Speaker and said, "I need your email address. I have a video to send you. Tell me if any of these guys are part of the group you know."

The detective gave him his email. After the call ended, Lucas sent the video to him.

She loved that efficiency and can-do attitude. Hell, she'd always loved that about him. It still blew her away to think she was sitting here with him. She'd been afraid she'd never get this opportunity again.

Ten minutes later there was a phone call. Lucas again put on Speaker, yet turning down the volume, including her in the update. So much easier to keep track when all the information wasn't secondhand.

"Okay, now you're in the middle of the hot spot," the detective said. "And I'm really not happy Andy is there."

"I know," Lucas said. "What do you want me to do?"

The detective paused. "We need to know where they go from there," he said. "I'll send two undercovers down. You're at the coffee shop, I presume, on the corner of Blackwell and Kitchener?"

"Yep," Lucas replied.

Tanya settled back, happy that maybe they wouldn't be alone on this job.

"Okay," the detective said. "Sit tight. Let us know if any of the men get up and leave."

"Will do," Lucas said. He ended the call. "Thanks for the video. I'll send it to my boss, plus we've got the local cops involved now," he said in a low voice.

She nodded slowly, looked at him and asked, "Is there any reason not to trust the detective?"

He shot her a look and a half smile. "Well, at least

you've learned something over all these years, and that's not to trust everyone," he said. "For now I do. He seemed pretty angry about Andy being in the picture with several other men well-known for dogfighting. So we are definitely in the right area. What we have to do now is figure out where these guys live."

Tanya rolled her eyes. "How the heck will you find that out?"

"The detective is looking it up. He'll likely see if he has names he can match with properties. But my priority is still finding Top Hat."

She frowned. "I hope it does not lead to doing anything dangerous."

"Really?" he asked, leaning forward. "Aren't you the one who just walked by those men to take a video of them?"

She shrugged. "But I'm in a public place."

"The next time you may not be," he warned.

She glared at him, but he was right, and she knew it.

LUCAS WAITED FOR the detective to get back to him. He also knew two plainclothes men were coming in soon enough, but it wouldn't be fast enough if these men split up and disappeared.

Lucas sent a text. **What are the addresses for the men?**

The answer came back. **We're right in the middle of their addresses. Can't give up private information like exact addresses, but two are on Blackwood and two others on Kenwood.**

Lucas pulled up his GPS on his phone and looked for

the two streets, Kenwood and Blackwood, on the map. Neither were terribly long streets, and all were within a few miles from where they sat. He studied the layout of the properties, looked at the men and said to Tanya, "I need to disappear. I wish there was some place to stash you."

"Why don't I sit at the counter while you do a little reconnaissance mission." Standing, she picked up her cup and walked to the front counter and sat down. Several women were there and a bunch of newspapers. Tanya motioned to the waitress to refill her cup. and she grabbed a newspaper.

Lucas got up, walked to the men's room but slipped out the back and headed for Kenwood Street. It was connected to Blackwood. He'd check out a couple properties as they were close.

Only three properties were found on this street, and all were fairly decent sizes. He could see from the satellite they had lots of room for animals. He hit the closest one. He found no sign of anyone on the property, and he slipped into the barn, moving his way down, but everything was empty. No signs of dogs or horses.

He went through all the outer buildings, but nothing was here—short of the kennels and a dogfighting ring being underground. And yet, why would there need to be anything underground when so much space was aboveground?

He carried on to the next property. Again found nothing but also nobody home. Maybe these people had full-time jobs, and it was a weekday—no, it was a Saturday. Maybe they were all out shopping. Frowning, he carried on to the third one, and this was definitely not uninhabited. Two men were working with horses, but the horses were jumpy. Lucas walked along the back fence, just out of sight, trying to keep an eye on them.

Dogs would make horses skittish, but there had to be a lot of dogs for dogfighting. As he walked around farther, he could hear several dogs howling. He kept walking and came upon three of the biggest, meanest, ugliest-looking things tied up with chains at the back corner fence. He stopped and studied them, seeing the aggression, the anger, the pain, noting the old wounds and nodded. "Well, there's three of them," he said. "Where the hell is Top Hat?"

He took several photos and sent them to the detective. Then he backtracked to the second property, but he saw no sign of dogs, chains or anything as he walked the perimeter of the fencing. Frowning, he returned to the first one but, walking the perimeter, found nothing.

He moved across the street and worked through that side of the block. The fourth property had a huge arena, and he found a kennel full of dogs too. Some of them were injured, tied up, and some were loose. He then went into another building, and, sure enough, there were cages full of small dogs.

He snapped as many pictures as he could and sent a text to Detective Madison. **We need to raid this property and save these dogs now. Before tonight.**

He got an answer back. **Animal control has been contacted. We're on it.**

He gave the address and slipped onto the next property. This one didn't appear to be much different. But there were no animals. He kept going and found one more property with two big dogs—a Doberman and a rottweiler—both bleeding and lacerated, with bad temperaments. He took pictures and texted them to the detective.

He walked back to the coffee shop and slipped in the front, as if from the truck, and walked to Tanya at the counter. He sat down beside her, ordered another coffee.

She raised an eyebrow and pointed out an article in the newspaper on rising property prices in the area. But he just nodded. In a low whisper, she asked, "Any success?"

He nodded. "Some."

She frowned. "That's too bad. Guess I was hoping we would be lucky and not find anything."

"Not finding something," he said, "is not an option."

"Maybe we can save some of them."

"Some, yes. All, no." He shook his head. "Not sure we can save some of these. Too far gone."

She stared at him in horror, and he shrugged. "It happens. But I'm not saying that yet."

"Top Hat?"

He shook his head. "No. If Andy is still here, I'd like to go back and search his place." He gave a nonchalant glance over his shoulder. But Andy was no longer seated at the table with his buddies.

She stared at Lucas, stood, called the waitress over. "How much do I owe you?" The waitress told her, and she put down the money. They walked out together just as Andy exited the men's room and returned to his table.

"Andy's back at his table, and his truck is still here," Lucas said with relief. "Let's go see if we can do a quick search of his place before he gets back."

"Do you really think Top Hat's still there? While you went looking for him, Andy had the very dog you were looking for hidden?"

"I don't think it's a case of *still there*," he said. "I think, if Top Hat was shot by Andy, then Top Hat was taken back there."

"That would really suck."

"Yes, it would. If I find Top Hat, I don't care. I just want him good enough to travel, so we can get the hell out of here. Get him to a vet if he's injured and get him home or at least to my sister's place. I'll figure out what I'll do after that."

"You'll take him yourself?"

Silence.

She looked at him. "Lucas?"

"I'm not sure what I'll do," he said with a note of finality. "It's too early to tell."

He might not know what his future plans were for sure, but he was already considering helping out Meg and Nathan with the kids and the dogs at their place. Then Lucas could pinch hit for Titanium Corp too as needed. But he didn't have the whole picture yet. He glanced at Tanya. It was up to her. However, now Lucas's immediate focus was on heading back to Andy's and doing a quick search. He didn't know when the undercover detectives would arrive here in town, but Lucas already planned to send a text telling the detective what his current plan was. Just before he went to hit Send, he stopped himself.

An inner urging said he didn't know who to trust yet. With Andy safely at the coffee shop, Lucas needed to get to Andy's place as fast as possible and find a way to park so nobody saw his vehicle.

"Where will you park?" Tanya asked as they drove across town.

"I was just wondering that. A neighbor's not too far away where we could park nearby. Then I could sneak over to Andy's place and search. We still don't know for sure that Andy has anything to do with this either. He just happens to be in a very good position to facilitate dogfighting."

"I hope you kill him," she stated bluntly.

He shot her a startled look.

"Okay. So, maybe not kill him, but he shouldn't be allowed to hurt animals."

He nodded but said nothing. His mind was busy trying to figure out the best way to get up to Andy's without being seen. The problem was, Andy had a long driveway, so if he came home when Lucas was parked up there, Andy would know he'd been here.

He frowned. "Andy left while you were still at his house, so maybe I can just park there and hope Andy doesn't come back while I'm out on his property."

"But that's taking a chance," she warned.

"True but short of parking somewhere a long way away and taking an hour to hike in, which will take time I don't have," he said, "there's not too much choice here."

"If he does come back, I can stay in the truck and tell him that you went looking for him."

"That would work," he said. Inside though, he worried. "As long as Andy doesn't appear to be too aggressive."

"He was always friendly before. And he did walk out of the house and leave me alone. So he obviously didn't think there was anything for me to find, even if I had cared to look."

"Or maybe the need to tell somebody else you were there was stronger," he said.

"There are phones for that," she said in a dry tone.

He chuckled. "True enough." He drove steady for a good fifteen minutes before they got to Andy's place; still no other vehicles were here. Lucas parked as close to the same spot as he could, then said, "I won't be long."

He shut off the engine, hopped out, left her with the

keys and took off. He didn't even bother going through the house. He headed for the barns and the dog pens. The fact that Andy was supposedly running dog training and rescue for large dogs gave him a good cover. Lucas didn't want to think ill of Andy, but he wasn't sure what else to do.

Lucas searched everywhere, and, with relief, he finally came back and realized there were no signs of any dog-fighting. Didn't mean Andy wasn't supplying dogs for the trade, but Lucas hadn't seen any signs of abused animals being kept there. But it also left him at a dead end as to where he was supposed to go from there.

He returned to the truck and hopped back in, shaking his head. "I didn't find anything." He put it in Reverse and drove down the driveway and back onto the main road, this time going in the opposite direction from which they came.

He studied the properties as he drove by, then contacted the detective, putting the call on Speaker. "Does Andy own just one piece of property? Or is there a second one somewhere?"

"A good question," the detective replied. "He does have a lot of land up there."

"I took a quick look, but I didn't see anything at his main property," Lucas said. "That's why I'm asking if there's another title somewhere."

"Doing a land search right now," the detective said.

"A lot of land is out here," Lucas said. "And just enough houses to keep things confusing."

The detective chuckled. "Isn't that the truth? He has another property about two miles away from the house you were in, and the far corner of this property touches the far corner of the other one, so there's probably a gate letting him go from one to the other one."

"Address?" The detective read it off, and Lucas punched it into the GPS. He pulled off to the side of the road, did a quick U-turn and headed back the way he had come from. "I've got it," he said. "I'll take a look to make sure nothing's going on there either."

"We've got a couple men already getting into position at the areas you were talking about earlier, and animal control should be there any time now."

"Good. You will need boarding for the dogs. There's probably around twenty dogs that I saw, and that's without counting the ones in cages."

"We've got various animal agencies alerted," the detective said. "You be careful though. A lot of criminal charges stem from something like this, and people get a little irritated over the thought of being locked up for a few years. Not to mention losing assets to cover their legal fees."

"I hear you," Lucas said. "I'd get a little pissed myself. I'm still looking for my dog, and I'm afraid he's already been worked into the system."

"I hope not," the detective said. "That would be bad news for him."

"And for anybody else. Top Hat's got an issue. Remember?"

"Right," the detective said with a heavy sigh. "Stay in touch. Let me know. You realize you're trespassing the minute you go on their property, right?"

"What property?" Lucas asked cheerfully. And he ended the call. He glanced over to see Tanya staring at him in surprise. "What?"

"He just brought up a good point," she said. "Trespassing."

"Yep," he said. "But if I don't, who will?" he asked.

"They could kick you out of the country."

"They could," he said. "I've got to go home anyway."

"Oh," she said quietly and settled back. "You weren't planning on going back a year ago."

"A year ago, we were getting married. I had a job lined up here and family close by. I was near the end of my naval commitment and all ready for a new beginning. And I would then start immigration proceedings, but remember? Something changed in that process."

"Yeah, the family part," she said sadly.

"I still want a family," he said. "That hasn't changed."

"You know that, even when you do get to that stage, there's no guarantee you'll have your own children."

"I didn't say they have to be my own, but it does feel very much like I would like to try."

"And if you can't?"

"Well, at that point, I'll have to see. An awful lot of children could use a good solid family."

"So you'd adopt?"

"I'm not against it," he said. "Will you be alone for the rest of your life?"

She swallowed hard. "I hadn't planned on it."

"No," he said. "But, if you're not prepared to have your own family, you have to find somebody who doesn't want one either."

"Lots of people don't want kids," she said. "And more so every day."

"Maybe," he said with a shrug. "But I'm not one of them."

And that note of finality in his tone had her gasping. "So, I guess we're not getting back together then, are we?" she asked with a broken cry.

He never said a word. In the back of his mind, he had no idea that she was even thinking along those lines. "Is that why you came with me today?" he asked. "Has your stance changed?"

"I just told you no," she said, sagging against the corner of the truck.

"You never did really explain why you don't want a family."

"Yes, I did," she said wearily. "I explained many times. You just didn't understand."

"I guess that's true," he said. He kept watching the GPS as he drove, following the directions. "It should be around here somewhere. The thing is, they weren't your children. They were your siblings, and I get that you felt like you didn't get a childhood because you spent it raising them, but that doesn't mean raising your own will feel the same."

"No," she said. "But I don't know that it'll feel any different either."

"You're too scared to try?"

"It was a lot of work," she said. "I had nightmares about failing. Nightmares that something would happen to them under my watch. I couldn't sleep. I couldn't rest, worrying about them."

"Ah," he said. "So it's not that you're worried about the work but more that you're afraid you won't be there to protect them all the time?"

"I was a lousy parent," she snapped. "Why would I want to repeat it?"

"*You* weren't a parent," he said. "That's what you keep getting confused about. You were an older sibling charged with a responsibility that shouldn't have been yours. *Your mother* was a terrible parent."

"No argument there," she muttered.

"You haven't separated your childhood from mother-hood."

"Because it seemed like one and the same," she said. "All I did was change diapers, warm bottles, feed kids, do laundry and chores."

"Do you really think it will be like that when it is your own children?"

"I don't know," she said. "I just have such terrible memories."

"I think it's got nothing to do with raising kids," he said. "Granted two parents raising kids has got to be easier than a single parent raising kids. But I think, for you, it has more to do with being afraid you will end up the same as your mother."

He heard her gasp. He nodded and said, "That's something you've refused to look at. But just because your mother was a piece of shit doesn't mean you'll be too."

Her small, gentle voice damn near broke his heart when she said, "But what if you're wrong? What if I am? I could never forgive myself if I ended up being just like her."

CHAPTER 7

I T SOUNDED SO much worse coming out of his mouth than from her own tortured thoughts. Tanya sagged back in the seat and said, "It's easy to dismiss. But what if ..."

"Now you're just borrowing trouble. Don't do that. This isn't the time or the place for this discussion." He took a left-hand turn and said, "This is our destination." He pulled up the long driveway to Andy's other property, and thankfully there were no vehicles and no house, but there were several outbuildings.

He nodded. "This looks like a likely prospect. You stay here." He shut off the engine and hopped out, leaving her alone to her thoughts.

She stared at the man she'd always loved as he walked away from her. How many times had he walked away from her? And yet, she knew it was her fault every time. Was he right? Was she more terrified about being a lousy mom than reliving her lousy childhood? It seemed too simple. Seemed too easy. It made her wonder if that was possible. Because, if it was, that would be a whole lot easier to deal with.

Her mother was still alive, but Tanya had nothing to do with her. The moment she could walk away, she had. And, of course, the guilt from that had been horrific too. Because all her siblings had been there looking to Tanya to be a mother. She did keep in contact with them, but the two youngest hardly even knew her.

When she'd left, the twins had been four. And now they were young teens, both boys and into their own lives. But the five siblings above them had all been girls. Tanya did keep in contact with them somewhat. The two closest to her in age were in college, and they talked regularly. She was very grateful for that bond—the others she talked to sometimes, but much less so. Those two girls were working instead of going the college route.

As for her mother, Tanya had very little to do with her. She pulled out her phone and checked her contacts. Her mother's was still there. Made her wonder just how long it had been since she'd last spoken to her. On impulse, she hit Dial. When her mother answered the phone, she said, "Hi. It's Tanya."

"Wow," her mother said in a snide voice. "What do you want?"

Tanya laughed. "I don't want anything. It just occurred to me that I haven't spoken to you in a long time, and I thought I'd see how you were doing."

"I'm alive. Now you know," her mother said, her tone suddenly weary. "So you can hang up and disappear again."

"I just might do that," Tanya said. "The fact is, hearing the way you speak to me, that tone, is enough to make me disappear for another five years."

"Good," her mother replied. "You were pretty damn useless anyway."

Tanya gasped and felt her blood boil. "Are you serious? I lost my childhood because of you. You were never home. Always out drinking with your buddies, getting banged by your latest conquest, leaving me to raise your family. I didn't want to be a parent. *That was your job.*"

"Maybe," her mother said. "But getting banged, as you called it, is what put food on our table. You think I liked having all those strangers crawl all over me? I didn't. But it doesn't matter. Down to the last two and pretty soon they'll be gone too."

There was an odd note in her mother's voice. Tanya sank back against the seat and stared out the window in the direction Lucas had gone. "Are you telling me that you only turned tricks to put food in the table?"

"What do you think I did it for?"

"Your next drink, your next shot of drugs," Tanya said. "There was never any food."

"You went to the food bank. You were fine."

"I could only go to the food bank so many times in a week," Tanya said. "Besides, it wasn't up to your eldest child to go to the food bank to pick up food for her siblings."

"So you're still bitching about your childhood."

"What are you doing with your life now?" Tanya asked. "Still drugs, booze and more men?"

"No," her mom replied. "I am trying to figure out what to do with your brothers."

"What's wrong with them?"

"They will need a home soon," she said. "And don't act like you don't know. It's not like you've reached out to take them."

"Take them? I don't even know them," Tanya said, everything inside her recoiling at the thought. "And why does somebody have to take them?"

There was a silence on the other end and then a bitter laugh. "Are you serious? You don't know?"

"Know what?" Tanya asked.

"I have stage four breast cancer," her mother said.

"Nothing doctors can do. I've got less than six months to live." With that, she ended the call.

Tanya stared at her phone as it crashed to her lap. It was one thing to hate your mother; it was another thing to hate your mother and then find out she was dying. But was she? Because Tanya couldn't trust anything that came out of her mother's mouth. How sad was it that the first thing she thought about after hearing a statement like that was how she was afraid her mother had just lied to get sympathy and money.

She sent her siblings a text, asking them. The older two didn't know anything about it because they hadn't had anything to do with their mom in years, just like Tanya hadn't, but the two younger girls confirmed it.

Six months was the first reply.

What about the boys still at home? Tanya texted.

No idea, wrote one.

Hoping somebody will take them. The reply from the other girl was more informative.

Not me, Tanya texted back.

Not you. But we don't know who else, her sister texted.

At that, Tanya stuffed her phone in her purse, crossed her arms over her chest and huffed. As if it would erase this recent phone call to her mother and her texts to her siblings. Why had Tanya even contacted her mother? She could have gone another five years without finding out more about her mother. Then she wondered if anybody would have told her when her mother passed.

Under her breath, she swore loud, long and fluently. When she was done letting all the anger out, she sagged deeper into the seat and pinched the bridge of her nose. She was damn sorry for her mother because she'd had a shitty life.

Tanya didn't even really know much about her mother's childhood, her upbringing, but when her one and only husband had taken off on a job that had him running across the country as a trucker, it seemed like he left her pregnant every time. And, somewhere along the line, the last two kids weren't even her father's because her father had died in an accident when her mother was pregnant with the fifth girl. But still, her mother had managed to pop out the twins—even though her mother had no clue who the father was.

Maybe the father should come into play. She pulled her phone back out and texted, **What about their father?**

Any idea who he is? Her younger sister's text was followed by a happy face emoji.

No, I don't, Tanya replied.

And she really didn't.

She tried to cast her mind back to think about who had been in her mother's life back then, but there'd been so many men.

How old are the twins now? She texted her sister.

Fourteen was the response.

"Shit," she whispered. And she shoved her phone back in her purse. But the story had gotten out now. There was no shoving it back into the recesses of her mind. What the hell was she supposed to do? Some of Lucas's words came back to her. Was it that she hated being a parent, or was it that she hated the thought of failing as a mother?

It was failing as a mother.

Because she'd already failed as a sister. She'd walked away. She couldn't handle it anymore—she had walked away and gone to college.

She had barely stayed in touch, shoving the responsibility back where it belonged—right on her mother's shoulders. Her mother had picked up the pieces and become a parent again. Maybe Tanya should have walked away a long time ago.

She lifted her head to lean back against the headrest and spotted Lucas heading toward her, talking on the phone. As he hopped in, he turned on the engine and peeled out of the driveway before she had a chance to even ask him what was going on. "What's up?"

"Andy's on his way," he said. "I saw him from the other side, leaving his second property. I'm pretty sure he's coming here because he saw me."

"See anything over there?"

"Oh, yeah," he said. "Dogs in all stages of health, some are pretty rough. But I need backup, especially if Andy's coming because he probably will not be alone this time."

"Should you call the detective?"

"I did. I also put in a call to 9-1-1, in case the detective isn't who I'm hoping he is."

At that, she gasped. "You're thinking he might be involved?" That was nothing she wanted to contemplate.

"It's a pretty big dogfighting ring," he said. "I wouldn't be at all surprised if some cops are involved."

"That's disgusting," she cried out, her heart aching at the thought.

He nodded as he turned left and raced down toward the neighbor's driveway and parked a ways down the road, hidden in a small copse of trees. "I want you to stay here, and I'll go back and see if I can't confront Andy."

"What?" she stuttered. "No. No. No. You can't do that." She reached out and grabbed his arm. "You'll get hurt."

"Maybe," he said. "But we must protect those dogs."

She swore. "Then I'm coming with you."

He shook his head. "Absolutely not. This isn't what you signed up for."

"It doesn't seem to matter what I signed up for," Tanya said. "If I can help, I will."

"Not this way." He had hopped out but now studied her face as she remained inside the cab. "What's going on? Did something happen while I was away?"

She shrugged. "Go. We'll talk later."

She watched as once again he took off. Luckily he seemed to be headed to ground nearer to where she was and farther from Andy's driveway. Yet she couldn't see the pens. Must be a tiny valley or recessed area. Maybe even a dried-up pond or whatever. As soon as he was out of sight, she slipped from the cab, the keys in her pocket, and headed up the road. She could see three vehicles coming in Andy's driveway. None of them looked to be cops.

She called Lucas. "You've got three trucks coming up Andy's driveway."

"I see them," he said. "I'm just about to let all the dogs loose. There are pens in the back. I'm trying to get into them."

"What if some of the dogs are aggressive?"

"I don't think it will be an issue," he said. "Six more dogs are in crates that I can't even get to sit up."

"I think a cop car is coming now," she said. "It's heading up the driveway behind them." She ran through the trees. "I'm approaching through the trees," she said. "I'm not close enough, so I can't hear what they're saying."

"Don't get any closer," he hollered into the phone.

She could hear dogs barking in the background on the

phone. And then there were shouts from the gathering of men on the driveway. "What the hell's going on?" She moved in closer, and, sure enough, there was no sign of the cop.

"Watch out," she said. "I think the cop might be with them."

"Shit," he swore. "You stay hidden. Do you hear me?"

"I do," she said. "You stay safe." All she got for an answer was a dead phone.

LUCAS COULD SEE the men approach from the driveway as he worked on freeing the dogs in the last two cages. The dogfighting men on foot and not knowing exactly where he was, gave him some time. As soon as he could free the dogs, they would all be out in the backfield. Then he just had to open up the fence to the other property, and they could get through. What he needed now was the police. The real ones.

He called the detective. "There's a cop here, and he's involved, so, if you're not involved, you sure as hell better be on your way."

The detective yelled, "Don't you get involved. I have backup coming, but it'll be a couple minutes."

"You don't have a couple minutes," Lucas said. "I've released about sixty dogs, and some of them need major medical assistance." He didn't dare study the animals too closely, or he'd lose it. Some were barely mobile. "You can hear the mob of men in the background. There are three vehicles and a cop car parked out front."

"I'm about five minutes away," the detective said.

"You sure as hell better be on my side because I'll have

your head on a platter if you're not."

"Stop being a tough guy," the detective snapped. "I want these guys as much as you do, but, even more, I want to know what cop is on their side because we can't have this happening."

"They're coming now, so you better hurry." And, with that, he ended the call, then pressed Record on his phone as he worked to get the last of the dogs out. Behind those two cages was yet another one.

Top Hat. And he was lying down, with barely enough energy to whine. But a whine was better than a snarl.

Lucas dropped down in front of the cage. "Hey, Top Hat. You okay, boy?"

The dog looked miserable, drool coming from his mouth. It looked like his shoulder was torn with blood matted on his fur. Lucas talked to him in a calm voice as he moved away the other crates. He had to get Top Hat down the neighbor's property to his truck.

His phone rang again, Tanya telling him how more vehicles were coming up the road. He opened the crate with Top Hat, picked up the dog and headed to his truck. Not too long afterward he heard voices yelling again, probably because they found the pens were empty now, just as he arrived at his truck. He pulled down the tailgate with one hand, panting heavily, and loaded Top Hat into the bed and jumped in behind him. He pounded on the cab. "*Gooooo,*" he yelled. But before she could, four police cruisers came flying up toward them.

One stopped, but the others streamed by. The cop hopped out, and he said, "You Lucas?"

"Yeah, you David?"

He nodded. "What have you got there?"

"This is Top Hat. He needs a vet. He's been shot. You go get those assholes. There are dozens of dogs that need help. Make sure you catch the assholes on the other properties."

"We've got a huge net going down," David said. "Go to the vet and then check in with me."

Lucas nodded, pounded on the cab once more, and said through the open window, "I'll give you the GPS directions off my phone. Go, go, go."

CHAPTER 8

TANYA COULD HEAR him in the bed of the truck, calling his sister, trying to find a decent, reputable veterinarian in town.

He tapped the window and said, "Take a left two lights up."

She slowed, got into the left lane and turned as instructed. Following his directions, she came to a large parking lot. She parked, hopped out and ran to the back of the truck. "Oh, God, he looks terrible. How could they do that to him?"

"Yeah," he said, "I'm taking pictures, and then I'm going inside to the vet."

"I'll let them know." She ran for the door.

"Meg called ahead."

Tanya nodded and burst in through the door. "Hey, we brought in an injured shepherd from one of the dogfighting properties, and he is likely to be the first of many dogs to come."

The receptionist nodded. "We heard."

"Do you have a gurney or something? He's pretty banged up and probably can't walk in."

A vet tech came out with a large trolley. "If you can get him onto this, that would help."

Tanya led the way to the truck with the vet tech following. At the tailgate, Lucas had Top Hat ready.

The vet tech took one look and asked, "Is he aggressive?"

"Possibly," Lucas replied. "He was shot, so that might have an effect on his disposition."

The vet tech pulled something from her pocket and within seconds had it around the dog's snout. Top Hat didn't even flinch. "We'll keep the muzzle on him for now, for everyone's protection. He is probably in a lot of pain. Should I get something to knock him out first?"

"No," Lucas said. "Let's just transfer him."

Top Hat's body was limp and was slid onto the trolley without much fuss. He whimpered until he ran out of energy.

"Lead the way," Lucas stated. They each took a side and gently pushed it forward, Lucas comforting Top Hat the whole way.

Tanya had never heard Lucas so caring or seen him so careful as he maneuvered the dog through the doors and into the back room. Nobody tried to stop him; nobody tried to tell him to stay out. She wondered if anybody had taken a look at Lucas's face and realized it would have been useless.

As soon as they were in an examination room, the vet tech said to her, "You need to go out to the waiting room."

Tanya understood the sense of that but had no intention of leaving Lucas. She might not be able to do anything to help, but she wanted to stay with the man and his dog. As a compromise she stepped out of the way, near the door.

The vet tech looked to Lucas and said, "Do you have any control over the dog?"

"Hard to say," Lucas admitted. "I have some military War Dog training, but he has been treated badly."

Just then a vet came in. "I heard we may be getting a few

more animals in."

"Yes," Lucas said. "I released over sixty dogs so far today."

The vet looked at him approvingly. "How many were injured?"

"Some of them badly," he replied. "Between lacerations, what looks like broken legs and open wounds, a lot of banged-up animals."

"I keep hoping somewhere along the line I'll see the last dogfight victim." He looked at Top Hat. "This is a completely different case."

"I think he was shot," Lucas said. "He's a relatively new arrival. He jumped over a six-foot fence, and I'm pretty sure they tracked him down and shot him."

The vet tech whistled. "Bet the cops don't like to hear that."

"Why did they keep him?" asked the vet tech. as another vet joined them.

"No clue. But likely to put him in injured and to let the other dogs have a go at him," the vet said. "Unfortunately we've seen it a lot. Let's set up an IV line and get some fluids into him with pain meds and get an X-ray done to see what we are dealing with."

Lucas stepped back to let them do their work.

Tanya reached out a hand and touched Lucas. "Come with me to the waiting room. We'll be in the way, and they need to do their jobs."

He looked down at her hand and nodded as he slid his fingers in with hers, squeezing tightly. He turned to look back at the two vets and their helpers working on Top Hat. "Thank you," he said.

She wasn't sure they'd heard him, since they were so

intent as they worked on the dog.

Back in the waiting room, she sagged onto the bench, pulling him with her, and said, "It has been a hell of a Saturday."

"Yeah. It's late. The last thing they want is dogs in need like this showing up at this hour of the day. There's no way Top Hat gets to leave tonight, not after a bullet hole like that. He'll probably need emergency surgery."

The receptionist interjected. "Most of us won't leave tonight, not after hearing how many animals are coming."

Lucas nodded. "I'm the one who helped them escape, but the shape of some of those animals …"

As his words failed, Tanya wrapped an arm around him. "Come here. How about I pour you a cup of coffee while we wait?"

He nodded. "Sometimes I really hate people."

She nodded. "Hey, you and me both. Remember the reason why I don't want to have a family?"

He crooked his lips and tucked her in close. "I do," he said, leaning back and resting his head against the wall behind the bench. "When was the last time you talked to her?"

"About an hour ago," she said. "After you suggested I call her, I called to see how she was." She turned to look at him, to find that steady gaze of his studying her, looking for a reaction.

"And?"

"Got hit with another shot of reality," she admitted. "She's got stage four breast cancer, and there is nothing the doctors can do. She has about six months."

His eyebrow shot up. "What?" he asked. "Damn. That's shitty."

Tanya bent her head and mumbled, "Karma."

"I don't know. Either way it's a rough ending to her life."

"We didn't exactly have words but neither did we have a good conversation. I didn't know anything about the diagnosis, so I wasn't exactly culling my words before she blurted out the truth."

"You rarely hold back as it is."

"I hope I'm not mean regardless," she said quietly. "Although I don't think my call was what she needed today."

"How many kids are at home?"

"Just the twins—they're fourteen now."

"What about their father?"

She gave a broken laugh. "Nobody knows who he is. He's had nothing to do with them all these years. Neither have I. I'm as much of a stranger as their father is."

"Can one of the other siblings take them on?"

She shrugged, hating to consider all of them were in various stages of their own lives and not likely to need or have the opportunity to take them. "I don't know," she said. "My two oldest sisters didn't know anything about my mother's diagnosis—just the middle two sisters. And they didn't tell anyone."

"Your mother probably wouldn't let them. I'm sure she had a certain amount of pride."

"What does she have to be proud about?" Tanya exploded. "I get it. She had a tough life, and I hold a lot of grudges I'm trying to let go of … particularly now."

"Now is a good time to let it go because pretty soon you won't have the chance."

"Argh," she whispered. "That's not the way I wanted to look at this."

"If you want to make peace with your mother and your childhood," he said, his voice steady, "then I suggest you do it in the next six months."

She nodded slowly. As she was about to speak, several vehicles pulled up to the vet clinic. The receptionist stood up and said, "And here come the dogs."

Beside her, Lucas bolted to his feet and walked out to see if he could help. Tanya just stared as dog after dog came in, some walking, some being carried, some in cages. The receptionist, her face set in stone, sucked in her breath as she watched the parade of sad animals.

She separated them into various treatment rooms. Those that looked to be not as bad were left in the waiting room to be dealt with last. Lucas carried in a very large bulldog that looked like part of his jaw was damaged and also had signs of extreme scarring. He was in a cage and whimpering.

Lucas brought him in and set the cage on one of the benches beside the receptionist. In a low voice he said something about the jaw. Tanya couldn't quite hear what he was saying, but the receptionist nodded and said, "Bring him through."

He opened the cage and slid the dog out and carried it back.

Two cops arrived with cages of small dogs. Seeing the little animals in the cages brought tears to Tanya's eyes. She shook her head and turned away. By the time she turned back, they had also been moved to the back. She curled up on the bench wondering about the absolute nastiness of people and realized that, in her mind, she was still comparing her mother to this event as well.

Just because she'd been dumped with all the kids, she still hadn't been out on the streets, turning tricks like her mother. She wondered if that was why her mother had been with all those men all this time? Was it to put food on the table? She'd always heard that was the answer, but, in her own troubled mind, she'd figured it was because her mother was looking for the next hit. She'd been a drug addict and an alcoholic. That combination with kids was deadly. Plus she'd lied about everything. Came home high and drunk all the time; sometimes gone three, four days at a time. Whether that had contributed to the breast cancer, Tanya couldn't say and doubted her doctors would even venture a guess.

She may not have had the best childhood, but it wasn't the worst. She hadn't been beaten or turned over to an orphanage. So, for the most part, she'd done all right. They had made do. There was usually food, just not many choices. As she gnawed on her lip, caught up in her memories, Lucas disappeared into the back.

"I THINK THIS is the last one," Lucas said to the vet tech.

She nodded, brushed away a tear and got to work.

"I'm pretty sure every vet in town is getting hit with a bunch of dogs," Lucas said. "It was bad. Really bad."

The bulldog was eased onto an exam table. He stood trembling, obviously in a great deal of pain, then he lay down suddenly as if his legs couldn't hold him up anymore. Lucas stood beside him, gently stroking him and offering comfort.

The vet started an IV. "He's really dehydrated. That jaw will need surgery, but we need to get his pain under control, some fluids in him, X-rays taken, then add him into the surgery schedule."

The door was opened a crack, and the initial vet stepped in, took one look and sighed heavily.

Lucas looked at her. "How's Top Hat?"

"The bullet grazed him, so I stitched him up. The bone has taken a hit, but it looks like he will be okay. The X-rays didn't show any other damage."

"May I see him?"

"For a minute. He needs to rest," the vet replied.

Lucas passed through the open door and entered the bay with all the cages of animals. Top Hat was on a gurney with tubes and an IV attached. Lucas looked at one of the technicians and asked, "You want help moving him into a cage?"

"I want to keep an eye on him a bit longer," she admitted.

"Oh. Okay. How is he? If you can get him stable, I'll take him with me tonight. I got a cage, and I can keep an eye on him all night. Gives you one less to worry about."

"Maybe," she replied. "For right now though, he can't be moved until we check his vitals."

Lucas nodded. "If you can put me to work, do so."

"I think one of the cops was looking for you," said one of the techs working on two of the smaller dogs. "Maybe go find out what he wanted."

"Sure," Lucas replied. He headed out through the waiting room to the front parking area, where cops were talking on their phones. He stepped out and introduced himself.

One of the men reached out and shook his hand. "You're the one who gave us the heads-up on that property?"

"Yes, and about four others."

"Great. We conducted the raids and rescued sixty-four dogs so far."

"Good," Lucas said with satisfaction. "But how do we stop this from happening again?"

"Some suspects have been charged multiple times," the cop said. "This time they were pretty aggressive, as if somehow we had stopped some important fight."

"Not surprised," Lucas said. "They look like they're only after the bottom line."

"I don't know about that," the other cop said, putting this phone away. "For some, this is a sport, and a lot of people will do all kinds of things in the name of sport. We're still looking into a motive for the attacks on the girls."

"I suspect Claire might have overheard something, but until we can get someone to talk …" The cops nodded. Lucas added, "We need to make sure all the animals are safe and take down the men responsible so they can't do this again."

"That's for the cops, not you," the second officer said, giving him a hard look.

"Sure," Lucas said. "What about the cop involved in this?"

Both men stiffened. "Yeah, what about him?"

"He was up at Andy's house with the other guys. Did you track him down?"

The two men looked at each other. "Can you identify him?"

Lucas shook his head, but when one visibly relaxed, Lucas smiled, and he said, "Because you're him."

The cop flustered. "What are you talking about?"

"You are the only one who relaxed when I said I couldn't identify him."

"Not because it's me," he said, anger in his voice. "Because I know every cop personally, and I don't want to think about any of them being involved."

Lucas nodded, but his gaze never stopped searching. "I've got a photo of his license plate on my phone, so we'll find out soon enough."

"What? Wait. Hang on a minute. Are you sure?" The two cops crowded around him.

"Yeah," Lucas said. "I also sent it to the detective I was dealing with. I don't want it to be in the hands of just one person. I might send it to the media too."

"I'd appreciate it if you don't do that," the cop said. "We have a hard-enough time with public opinion without having anybody thinking we have bad cops running around."

"There's always bad cops," Lucas said, fatigue in his voice, "just like there are bad people in every other profession."

"Maybe," they said. "But it's not us. Anybody who would do this to the dogs, we don't want any part of. We want to know which cop is dirty, so we don't get caught up in the same mess."

He studied their faces for a long moment, turned to look at Tanya through the front window of the clinic, then walked around to the back of the two police vehicles and took photos of their license plates.

Only one protested. Lucas looked at him and said, "Every time you open your mouth, I think you're guilty."

That made the cop mad. He glared at Lucas. "I don't know who the hell you think you are, but you got no business making accusations like that."

"Maybe not," Lucas said. "But, in a case like this, somebody or multiple somebodies have been turning a blind eye to all of this for too long a time. Somebody keeps helping them get off, and that's got to stop. These animals have suffered, and those men are assholes." He brought up the images he had of the vehicles heading up to Andy's place and checked the license plates.

He glanced at the suspect cop to see his face creasing with worry again. "Interesting," he said. "You're still worried. So if it isn't you, you know who it is."

"Maybe it's you."

"I'll send it to both of you. Give me your emails."

And again, one cop hesitated.

"You really got a problem with this, don't you? Never mind. Here's the cruiser in question." Lucas held up his phone so both men could see it but focused on the one cop's reaction. Lucas saw the shock and fear on his face. He looked at the second officer. "You better grab hold of your buddy here. He's involved. In a big way."

"Hell no," the accused man blustered. "I don't know what you are talking about."

"Except for one thing," the second cop said. "That's your nephew. You do know what the hell is going on, don't you?"

The cop shook his head. "No. You know Ronnie's not a bad kid. He just got in with a bad crowd."

"He is a cop," Lucas said. "I don't care how many bad crowds he got in with. He. Is. A. Damn. Cop. Now. He is supposed to break up the bad crowds, not join in." Lucas sent another message to the detective. "Just in case you think this cop is free, he's not. I sent the information to the detective. I'm working with other detectives too, in case that one is bad news as well."

"If you're talking about Detective Madison, he's a good guy," the other cop said. "Straight as an arrow. He will clean this up in no time."

"Then why hasn't he?"

"He's been on it for the last couple months, but he suspected a murder was tied in with this. He was focusing on that. You've broken things wide apart. But I don't know that he'll thank you for it when he was trying to get to the bottom of the murder."

Lucas swore softly. "You're referring to Claire, aren't you?"

The cop's gaze narrowed. "You know her?"

He motioned toward Tanya inside the clinic and said, "They are best friends."

"You mean, *were* best friends," said the accused cop. "My nephew had nothing to do with that."

"If he's involved in one issue," Lucas said, "he is involved in both."

He watched the fear flare in the cop's eyes.

Lucas nodded. "It is already too late for your nephew. The question is, just how involved are you, and how many times did you turn a blind eye and let this shit happen around you?"

"You don't know anything about me," the cop blurted out.

Lucas nodded. "No, I don't, and I don't want to either." He snapped a photo. "Let's see what your face all over the news does." The cop now blubbering, Lucas turned away and walked back into the clinic. He sat down beside Tanya, hating that he felt so dirty and so angry.

"You okay?"

He wrapped an arm around her shoulders and rubbed her back. He had been so focused on his own feelings, he had forgotten about her and how difficult this must be for her. And she didn't even realize how much this was connected to Claire's death. "I will be," he said. "How are you doing?"

"Feel like shit," she muttered. "So much has gone on. It's overwhelming."

"I know. I'm sorry about your mom."

She nodded. "I am too. Because you're right. She's had a shitty life. I guess I was hoping, somewhere along the line, that she'd straighten up and find a few years for herself."

"Maybe you've misjudged the last few years. Maybe she's been good, and this is just a very sad, fast end for her."

"I don't even know what to think about any of it," she said, a yawn releasing. "I just want it all to go away."

"You should have stayed home today," he said abruptly. "I had no business bringing you into this."

"You didn't know it would become this," she said as she snuggled in close, her eyes closing. "The question now is, when can we go home?"

"Pretty soon," he said. "They are just checking Top Hat over. We might be able to take him home tonight."

She bolted upright. "Really?"

He nodded. "Really."

She beamed, and then her smile fell away. "I suppose you are going back to your sister's."

"Maybe," he said. "I have to take care of Top Hat."

"Right. He would probably be better off there."

"Maybe," he said. "Although there are two kids under the age of six living at Meg's place. He might not be the best around them. If I can get enough medication, maybe he'll sleep for a good twelve hours."

"We can go to my place, grab a few hours' sleep, and then go to your sister's place, if Top Hat is doing okay." She studied his face. "He might need to see another vet tomorrow."

"That might work," he admitted. "It's hard to say at this stage."

Just then the vet stepped out, looking very tired.

Lucas stood up. "You've got a long night ahead of you."

"I do. It's worse when we're short on space. I understand you are interested in taking Top Hat home with you?"

Lucas nodded. "Back to my sister's. Lots of space for him there."

"I don't suppose you have anything in writing to say this dog should go with you?" she asked delicately. "With everybody worried about stolen dogs, I feel like I need to do some due diligence."

"Would a couple emails help or a couple texts?" He swiped and scrolled and brought up an email from Corporal Badger and then Corporal Jager. "This might help clarify."

"Interesting," she said as she read them.

"Here. Let me call." He keyed in Badger's number and put the phone on Speaker as it rang. He told Badger he had found Top Hat. He told him the vet wanted to talk to him and took the phone off Speaker and passed her his phone. The vet had a short conversation and then handed the phone back.

"Good enough," she said. "You go get his cage, and we will get him ready, will prepare some medication."

Two more cops stood by, listening. "He's really one of the US War Dogs?" one cop asked.

Lucas nodded. "He's a K9 military dog that somehow got mixed up in this rescue shipment. And Andy, the great Andy, always on the lookout for dogs to fight, took him. Top Hat jumped a six-foot fence to get away from Andy. The dog must have known what a piece of shit Andy was.

Still, he tracked down my dog and shot him. That's the kind of guy you're protecting," he said with another hard look at the crooked cop.

The cop's face turned a deep red, but he didn't say anything.

Damn good thing he kept his trap shut because Lucas was ready to pop him one if he didn't.

CHAPTER 9

TANYA DROVE CAREFULLY. She knew Lucas wanted to drive, but he needed to stay beside Top Hat. They were both in the truck bed, and he was talking to the dog quietly in his cage, but with the door open, so he could run his fingers gently through his fur.

Top Hat was pretty drugged but conscious. His eyes were moving; she'd seen it for herself.

"Are we going straight to my place?" she asked through the open back window. "You never did decide."

"Yes," he said. "Though I'm tempted to take him to a vet in town."

"I don't think he needs a vet," she said. "He's been well cared for. He just needs to heal. But tell me something."

Lucas lifted his head so she could see his face in the rearview mirror. "What?"

"How do all those dogs get the help they need?"

"What do you mean? You just saw the vets and their assistants working after hours back there on these poor animals."

"But, I mean, who pays for all this? I'm worried there won't be enough charitable donations for all of them."

Lucas nodded, glanced at her in the rearview mirror again, then focused on Top Hat as he spoke to Tanya. "Well, of course, Titanium Corp paid fully for Top Hat here." He gave the dog another soft stroke. "And I'm sure, like in other fields, a certain amount of pro bono services are given."

"But for sixty-four dogs?" she asked, pressing the point. "And that's not the only vet clinic around."

"Yeah, I see what you mean."

"And, like the vet said, it happens over and over again. It's not like this is a one-time event."

"You're right." He shook his head, then continued, "Even Titanium Corp works off donations. We have one guy, the father to a buddy SEAL, and a veteran SEAL himself, Gunner Redding, who keeps us running mostly, but he also steps in when the needs are even greater. Like here. He donated money to these local vets. He'll call around and get more donations to see that the veterinarians are reimbursed and that no animal is turned away simply because a bill is not paid.

"If that doesn't cover all the dogs just for tonight's vet bills, I don't know how it works in Canada. In the States, we have special governmental agencies and even grants that can help out. Despite the fact that some of our homeless animals end up here more often than they should, America is full of animal lovers. They donate their time and their money to worthy causes in all countries. Plus, as former SEALs, we have a special brotherhood all over the world that we can call on to help in various ways. If not with money, then with time, contacts, supplies …"

"Same here, I just don't know if there's enough for a big influx like tonight. I hope so. I want to know the vets involved tonight at all the animal clinics will most likely be paid. So that these poor dogs can live a better life."

"That's the plan, yes." He smiled at her. "I know some people I can ask to help out."

Her eyes lit up. "Good." "It's *very* good. Now keep an eye out and make sure we're not being followed, okay?"

Her gaze darted to the rearview mirror. "That's really not a cool thing to say to me," she exclaimed.

"We could also find somewhere halfway between," he said.

She considered it. "It's already eight p.m. We can pick a hotel for the night, if you want, and get some food."

"Yeah. Let me do some searching and see what I come up with."

In her rearview mirror, she could see him pull out his phone and start tapping away. How the world had changed for them. Everybody was on the internet—hotels, restaurants, gas stations—from here to home, all online.

She kept driving with a vigilant eye on her surroundings. She loved to drive—she was really happy in a vehicle doing road trips. Either as a driver or a passenger, it didn't matter. But now, knowing she had Lucas and Top Hat in the bed, well, there was a certain amount of contentment in this trip. She hadn't expected it—the bonding together. She had more hope for them now.

He was still an American citizen, so they'd have paperwork to deal with. He had been badly injured, and there would be a lot of questions and potentially some health adjustments. Not that she'd seen anything that had slowed him down. If she hadn't known he was injured, she couldn't tell. So really what she was doing was throwing up minor roadblocks, assessing them, and then tossing them away.

"Any luck?" she asked, studying him in the rearview mirror. His head was down.

"We can stop off in Torino," he said. "A couple bed-and-breakfasts are there and a couple of motels. A motel might be better. We can drive right up to the door, and I can unload Top Hat."

"Do we tell them we have a dog?"

"I'll probably talk to the manager about that," he said. "We have an injured dog that won't get out of his cage, so it's not like the same dog damage of a dog that's bouncing on beds and peeing everywhere."

"Yeah, don't we have to take Top Hat out to do his thing too?"

"I'm not sure," he said, looking at the dog. "He's pretty well out cold."

"That's the best way for him to stay as long as he's healing," she said.

"Exactly," Lucas said. "You've got another twenty-five minutes roughly, and then we can stop and see."

"Otherwise, we can go straight home," she suggested again.

"Let's take a look at how we feel after dinnertime."

Buoyed by that thought, realizing it really wasn't that far to the next break, she said, "What do you think I should do about my mother?" Her question came out of the blue, she knew, and there was absolutely no right answer here, but she wanted to hear his input.

"I think you should call her. Go see her and see if she needs help," he replied.

She laughed. "That didn't take you long to reply."

"There really isn't much to figure out," he said. "She is still your mother."

"I don't want to get too close. I know that makes me a horrible person. But every time I've been close to my mother, I've been badly burned."

"Remember to walk in her shoes for a little bit and try to

be more understanding," he said. "I'm not judging because that's not what this is about. I don't know what I would do if my sister had stage four cancer, but I would be there for her. No matter what."

"Sure, but your sister also didn't give you the worst years of your life," she said with a sigh. "Never mind. I'm still hanging on to my grudge, aren't I?"

"Yes," he said. "Time to let it go."

There was such a note of humor in his voice that she laughed. "If only it was that easy ..."

"I don't think it's much harder," he said gently. "Just like when I was injured and had to deal with the loss of my foot. For many people it would be traumatic. I looked at it and said it could be so much worse. It could have been a whole leg, could have been both legs, and then what would I do? This is a foot and a prosthetic. Big deal. It is not the end of the world."

"Meaning my childhood could have been much worse?" She caught his nod in mirror. "I was thinking of that earlier today. I didn't have to do tricks out on the street with her. Although I did use the food bank as much as I could, the neighbors gave us a lot of extras. My mother did still cook."

"I think the trick here is to realize she did what she could. Yes, she was a drug addict, and, yes, she was an alcoholic, but her life is different now. She's on the last few steps of whatever path she has for herself, and I'm sure there's got to be some guilt over the path she took. Now might be the time to get that all settled."

That comment made her feel something deep inside. "Maybe I'll call her again tomorrow."

"Do that," he said. "For all you know, she might want nothing to do with you either. But you need to find healing and closure for yourself first. If you happen to give her some closure as well, that's all to the good. Talk to your brothers. See what they want, and then walk away if that's what you want."

"My sisters and I have texted but I haven't had anything to do with the boys."

"Right, the new age," he said, laughing. "People prefer a cold objective text rather than dealing with a messy phone call. Or an even messier visit."

"It's the way of the world," she said.

"What will you do about your job?" he asked.

"Not a whole lot I can do," she said.

"The cop seemed to think Claire's and Alice's cases were connected. What are the chances your reputation smearing was also part of it?"

"*Hmmm*," she said. "If that's the case, why did I get off so easily?" she asked.

"Maybe they were afraid of getting caught. After all, three girlfriends getting hit at the same time would look too suspicious."

"Maybe they were saving the best for last, just biding their time," she said.

"The detective is still working that angle. And it's definitely something we should dig into deeper."

"Try finding out if anybody who worked at my company, or was associated with that company, has anything to do with this dogfighting ring. I wouldn't even have a clue about how to investigate something like that," she said.

"I can do some of it," he said. "We will need to get access to my computer."

Tanya put on her blinker and pulled into a restaurant parking lot. She wasn't at all surprised to see it was a steak and rib joint. Of all the things Lucas liked to eat, meat was at the top of the list. She parked where there wasn't any danger of somebody banging into Top Hat in the bed but which also gave them a bird's-eye view from the front window of the place.

She hopped out as Lucas opened her door. Then she took a closer look at the dog. "He doesn't look any different, does he?" she asked worriedly.

"No," he said. "He's holding his own though. He's just exhausted from these last days of hell. The longer he rests, the better he will be."

"I know. It's just hard to see an animal like this."

"It's worse for the ones we left back at the vet clinic," he said. "I've been getting texts from the cops. They managed to grab Andy and seventeen other men. They seized over 140 dogs total today."

She gasped. "Oh, my God. Wow!"

"They are going through all their records. Hopefully they got everyone."

"They get a slap on the wrist and carry on or what?"

"There will be cruelty against animals laws and gambling laws they've broken. I don't know what all they can do. This is your country. I don't know what we would even do in the US," he admitted.

"As long as the dogs were rescued," she said, "that's a big part of it."

"It'll take a lot of time and effort for them to be rehabilitated and then rehomed," he said.

Tanya stretched her arms above her head and twisted her neck, getting out the kinks.

Lucas shook out his arms and his legs, rotated his neck gently. He shut the driver's side door, held out his hand for the keys and locked up the truck.

"LET'S GO IN and have something to eat," Lucas said. "It's late. We've had a long day. We only have about an hour and forty minutes left if we go all the way home."

"Which I am a fan of," Tanya said. "It seems silly to stay here, and then go home in the morning. I don't mind driving longer. We can sleep in tomorrow."

He nodded.

Inside the restaurant, they were seated at the window where he could keep an eye on the truck. The waitress returned with coffee and menus, but he didn't even look at it. "I'll have a steak, baked potato, a big salad and lots of garlic bread."

The waitress chuckled. "Absolutely." She looked at Tanya.

Tanya smiled and said, "I'll have the same. Whatever I can't eat, he'll finish for me."

The waitress nodded and disappeared. Lucas hugged a cup of coffee in his hands as he contemplated their next move. "I'm afraid they're all connected to the dogfighting rings in your town," he said. "The police are specifically looking for a connection to Claire's murder. We have to expect dogfights are happening between here and there."

"This is a fairly small town," she said. "I don't think there's more than five or six thousand people living here. I'm surprised there was actually a steak house."

"I'm not," he said. "It's on the highway with a lot of truckers. Everybody knows they like to eat well."

"True enough," she said with a smile. "So how do we

find out if anybody else is connected here?"

"I don't know." He studied the dimly lit atmosphere. "It's still something that's hard to believe."

"That's what I felt like when I was sitting in the truck. It all felt so unreal," she said.

"But my brother-in-law heard about dogfighting rings near him," Lucas said. "He's been approached by a couple people to keep an eye out for aggressive dogs, not for safety but because breeders want them."

"Has he given the names of those people to the police?" she asked in a low tone.

He nodded. "He has, indeed." Just then the doors opened, and four men stepped into the restaurant. Lucas stiffened. "Don't look now, but those men are bad news."

"How do you know?" she asked, tilted her head. She didn't dare look at them directly.

"Because two of them were in the restaurant with Andy," Lucas said. "They've either been released or haven't been caught." He aimed his phone toward them and sent out several text messages to the cops he'd been working with. "I don't know if they're here because of us or if they're just here."

"They're coming our way," she whispered.

Not only did they come their way, but they stopped at the table.

"You did a stupid thing today," one of the men said.

Lucas looked up at him with a bland face. "I disagree. I found many injured dogs living horrible lives in tiny cages for the entertainment of a bunch of ingrates. Most of the dogs needed stitches and surgeries. They were a mess."

The men looked around, and two of them nudged the man who had spoken. "Joe, back off, man."

Joe stiffened at the rebuke and put his fists on the table, glaring at Lucas. "They weren't none of your concern," he snapped.

"They are everybody's concern," Lucas retorted, leaning into the man's face. Lucas wasn't backing down one bit. "*Joe, you better get your ass out of here before somebody kicks it for you.*"

He heard the other two men suck in their breaths and realized that, among them, Joe was probably known as the hard-ass and more likely to be the one to try to take Lucas down than to take a step back. That was okay by Lucas, he was bruising for a fight. He'd already put his back to the test carrying dogs, but he'd be damned if he'd take this shit lying down. If they wanted trouble they'd found it. But, as long as everybody else was aware Joe was making trouble, maybe his buddies would wise up and slip Joe out of this place.

Joe glared at him. "Again, it's none of your business, and, if you want to keep yourself and what you care about … safe …"

"Somebody stole my dog," Lucas said. "I've got him back now."

The man's face startled in surprise. "Is that the shepherd Andy had?"

"The cops let you out early or something? Do they know about you and stealing the dogs and Andy's big connection? Or did you manage to slip by the cops?"

One of the group slowly pulled away from them, turned and walked out of the restaurant, distancing himself from whatever happened next. *Smart man.* Too bad the others weren't following his lead. "Well, he obviously got wiser," Lucas said, pointing at the man leaving, "and doesn't want to get cornered with whatever this is going down."

"I spoke to the cops," Joe said in a snarling voice. "So what? They don't have anything on me."

"You from around here?" Lucas asked. "So, you just stop by to harass somebody having dinner?"

A second man left their group for the exit, leaving just one with the very vocal Joe.

"No, I'm not from here, but they know me. I come through all the time," he said as he pounded his fist on the table, making several patrons turn and look at him. "But I'll find out where you live. That's for sure. And her."

Joe turned to walk away with his last buddy. Instantly, Lucas was on him. He grabbed Joe's hands from behind him and started to squeeze, rubbing the bones tight and hard together—a grip he'd learned a long time ago.

"You will never, *ever* threaten her again," he said in a hard voice, pulling Joe closer. "You *ever* utter another threat like that, you won't wake up the next morning. Don't think I'm kidding. It's a fucking promise."

Joe just sneered at him, but it was hard to keep the sneer going when his hands were being crushed. Finally he nodded, and Lucas released him.

"Don't forget it," he said. "And, if you're involved in that dogfighting bullshit, I'll take you down with the rest of them too."

The man still with him slung his arms around Joe and forcibly removed him from the area. Lucas looked over to see Tanya trembling. He cussed and wrapped her up in his arms. "They won't get to you. I promise."

She shook her head. "You can't promise," she cried out. "You'll go back to your bloody life down South and leave me up here for those assholes. What the hell have I gotten myself into?"

The manager came to their table, his face contorted. "I'm so sorry for that scene. He's a known troublemaker in this area, but we've never had him go this far."

Lucas looked at him. "Does he live around here?"

The man shook his head. "He's about halfway from here to Red Deer," he said. He pointed out a couple trucks in the parking lot. "Those are theirs. They come in here all the time on their way through."

"Which one is his? Do you know?" Lucas asked.

"The black one," the manager replied. "With the big cab. I'll go check on your dinner," he said and turned away, heading for the kitchen.

Lucas got up from the table and walked outside. He took pictures of the two trucks' license plates, and those on either side of the pair of trucks, and sent them to the cops. Then he headed back inside. As he went to sit down, he caught Joe's glare. Lucas smiled at him, waved his phone and sat down across from Tanya. "That'll help too," he said.

"All you are doing is antagonizing him."

"He has to make a move, so I can slap him back down again," Lucas said quietly. "Otherwise, you'll live with that threat all the time."

CHAPTER 10

S HE WASN'T SURE how she was supposed to handle any of this, but they were back on the road again, and Lucas was driving. She'd hardly eaten. Her nerves and stomach had refused to accommodate her appetite. But he'd had no problem devouring his meal. They brought the leftovers for Top Hat for when he eventually got hungry.

"You shouldn't have egged them on," she said quietly.

"Maybe," he said with a nod. "But, with bullies like that, you have to let them know you are on equal ground. Otherwise, they just think they can lord it over you. And then we end up with bigger trouble."

"Will anybody come and deal with them?"

"The cops have been informed," he said. "I'm hoping they raided Joe's property while he was at the restaurant."

A truck went whizzing by them, way too close for comfort, but he held his ground. "And that was him," he said. He picked up his phone, hit a number and waited for a voice to come on the other end.

She didn't even want to listen, but she knew he was contacting the police. He kept looking in the rearview mirror. Finally she understood something was seriously wrong. "One's behind. One's in front."

"Sure," he said. "It's a sandwich. But I wasn't born yesterday."

He hit the brakes, pulled off to the wrong side of the road, where there was no oncoming traffic, and the guy behind him passed without having a chance to hit the brakes. Lucas pulled in behind him.

She smiled. "Well, that was smooth."

"Yeah, but what they're doing isn't," he said. He ended his call and tossed his phone on the seat beside him. "The cops have been alerted, and we'll see how far this goes."

She bit down hard on her bottom lip. "Why are they being such assholes?"

"They've been shaken because of the raids. Their dog-fighting ring was busted up, and they're afraid their status quo is about to get disrupted."

"How can they hurt dogs like that?" she muttered.

"I imagine most will get rehomed as soon as they're healthy. Dogs are also resilient. What we have to do is stop this from happening again, and the only way to do that is to make sure the men lose their properties and get jail time. They need to be on some permanent watch list, so they are monitored for the rest of their lives."

"I'm not sure what the laws are here," she said, "but, if they had anything to do with Claire's murder, that would make it much more serious."

"It would, indeed," he said. "Who knows? Maybe we'll get lucky and find some proof that nails every one of their asses to the wall."

It didn't seem like any time at all before he pulled up in front of her place. She looked at it and was surprised. "I didn't even realize we were this close."

"You're tired," he said. "It's been a long day." He hopped out, opened up the truck bed and gently pulled out the cage with Top Hat. She took the end he was holding, and Lucas went around to grab the end coming out of the truck. They both grunted when they had the full cage out. "What does he weigh, like one-forty?"

"I think so," he said.

They walked in tandem, keeping Top Hat level. "Good thing there was no sign of the trucks anymore. I was afraid they'd follow us home."

"Not once I got in behind them," he said. "I think that disturbed them more than they were comfortable with."

"It'd be nice if the cops got to them first."

"With any luck, they will," he said cheerfully.

She led the way down the hall to the stairs. "Damn. No elevator," she said on a laugh.

"Just keep going," he said. They huffed and puffed their way up to the second floor. They put the cage down at the door. Tanya took a few deep breaths as she slid her key in the lock. They pulled the cage into her apartment, Top Hat whimpering quietly. While she locked the door, Lucas bent down and opened the cage door and leaned in to check on Top Hat. "He doesn't look too bad," he said. "It'll be interesting to get him in and out to go to the bathroom."

"I know. I was thinking about that," she said. "You'll have to carry him."

"We'll see," he said. "He's still pretty out of it."

"Good," she said. "That's the way I'd like to be right now." She stood on her feet, swaying. "You good with the couch?"

"I'm fine with the couch," he said as he took off his jacket, kicked off his shoes and stretched out on the couch. She stared at him in surprise. "Don't you want a blanket or a pillow?"

"If you've got them, sure," he said.

She nodded, headed to her linen closet and pulled out a blanket and pillow, carried them to him. "See you in the morning." She walked past Top Hat, smiled down at the dog and said, "Sleep well, Top Hat."

In her room she took care of her evening ritual in double time and dropped face-first on her bed. She was beyond exhausted. She closed her eyes and drifted off to sleep.

LUCAS COULDN'T BELIEVE he was actually at Tanya's place. It was a different one than he'd been in before of course, but the place had never mattered to him. It had been all about her. They'd spent a lot of nights together, a lot of evenings together, making plans for their future, except for the one big issue always there between them. It wasn't the time to start thinking about that now because, unlike her, he was constantly on the lookout for anyone following them.

He had taken a couple corners to evade them, hoping they didn't know where she lived. If they did, it would be a mess. Even though he was confident nobody had seen him, he hadn't hidden his vehicle. He had parked it across the street. He knew he wouldn't sleep well because of that.

He drifted in and out a couple times. Sat up, checked the street in front, stood at the door, listening for any movement in the hall. No activity. Went back to sleep.

In the morning he got a text, waking him up. It was six a.m. It was one of the cops telling him they had raided three properties last night, and another twenty-four dogs had been recovered. The men from the restaurant were still at large. Lucas winced. "Great. Means they are probably looking for us, pretty hard-core," he mumbled to himself.

He dialed Detective Madison. When he answered, Lucas said, "Any chance they know who I am?"

"I don't know," the detective said. "We did raid these three properties, and I know we're not done yet. We're hoping to get a few more."

"Right," Lucas said. "I'll put my sister and brother-in-law on alert then to make sure. I've still got Top Hat, and we're at Tanya's place but will be heading over to my sister's soon."

"Good," the detective said. "Maybe get there a little earlier just to be sure. It'll be a long weekend as we'll still be searching as many of these properties as we can find."

"Good enough," Lucas said. He hopped up to put on some coffee, coaxed Top Hat out of his cage, and he seemed a lot more subdued. They slowly made their way down the stairs. Top Hat was a trooper, he barely whimpered. He took care of his business as Lucas looked around at the driveways and the parked vehicles.

No sign of the vehicles from the night before, and nothing looked different from when they had pulled in during the night. Top Hat was feeling a little more energetic as they made their way back inside.

"Probably hungry, right, boy?" Lucas asked.

When he opened the apartment door, Tanya stood there, an odd look in her eyes.

"I didn't want to wake you," he said. "I took Top Hat out to go to the bathroom."

"I was standing here, surprised to see the truck, thinking that maybe you had taken off again."

"Again?"

She shrugged. "It was part of our life together, wasn't it? You were always going off somewhere."

"Well, life has changed in that regard. I don't even have a normal job anymore," he said with a smirk. "I need to head back to my sister's place. The cops contacted me to say they've raided three more properties and have a few more they're looking into. And the four jerks from the restaurant are still at large. Wanted to make sure I kept an eye out."

She frowned. "Do they think they'll go to your sister's?"

"I don't know if anybody knows who I really am," he said, "but let's not take that chance."

"I'm coming with you then," she said.

"That's fine," he said. "You can. I did make coffee, but I figured, after that, I'd leave."

"*We* will leave," she corrected. She poured two cups of coffee. "Maybe I'll grab a quick shower."

He nodded. "I'll feed Top Hat the leftover steak." He cut the steak up into bite-size pieces and fed him by hand. The dog took it gently and chewed slowly. Lucas filled a bowl with water, and Top Hat seemed to enjoy that more.

When Tanya came back out with her long blond hair braided down one side, he thought of the number of times he had wrapped that braid around his hand and used it to pull her to him to kiss her. He forced himself to look away and take several long, slow, deep breaths.

"Are you okay?" she asked as she pulled on a sweater.

He nodded. "If you're ready, we can leave now."

"I had one cup of coffee. I'm good to go," she said.

"In that case, let's leave." He walked over to Top Hat, who was lying in the cage. Lucas bent to close the door and whispered, "Let's go, boy." But Top Hat didn't want the door closed. He got up and stepped out of the cage.

"Are you okay to walk?"

Top Hat's tail thumped the ground. There was no sign

of aggression. He was more than happy to leave.

Lucas hooked the leash on him, lifted the cage with one hand and led the dog from the apartment. They walked over to the truck, Tanya trailing behind. Lucas loaded the cage in the bed and walked back up to Top Hat. He was still wagging his tail.

"Okay," Lucas said. "We'll try it your way." He helped him into the back seat and waited until Tanya got in front and climbed into the driver's side. He looked at Tanya. "Ready?" he asked her.

She nodded. "As much as I will be. While Meg and I talk a lot, I haven't seen your whole family in a while," she admitted.

"Well, they're not scary," he said. "Let's go make sure they're all okay."

She nodded. It was a fifteen-minute drive. When he pulled up, his sister stepped out and waved.

"Glad to see you back," she said cheerfully. "Everybody doing okay?" Her gaze was on Tanya.

Tanya smiled and nodded. "Yes," she said. "Everything is good."

Relief washed over Meg's face, and she broke into a bigger smile.

Lucas looked from one to the other and said, "Yes, things are okay." He opened the back door and helped Top Hat out. The dog shook out his fur and sniffed the air as he walked slowly in the house with Lucas.

Nathan was seated at the kitchen table but stood up when Lucas and his dog entered the house. Nathan smiled and said, "I figured you'd find him."

"I found him, but he was shot."

His sister was behind him and gasped out loud. "Oh, the

poor dog."

He sat down and explained everything that had gone on. Top Hat sat down, then slowly slid to a lying position beside him. He looked down and gently stroked him on the top of his head. "He's been through a lot."

"Those damn dogfighting rings," Nathan grit out.

"They carried out raids on three more properties," Lucas said. "We had some ugly business at the restaurant last night. Now the police are concerned about me, about you."

"Let me go check on the dogs," Nathan said.

Top Hat lifted his head curiously but slowly stood, as if not sure what was happening.

"I'll go with you, Nathan," Lucas said. "You girls stay inside, okay?"

His sister looked at him worriedly. "Okay," she said. "You take care."

He nodded, and Lucas and Nathan headed outside. They checked all the pens. "Looks good. For—"

A weird ping hit the barn, and they both ducked instinctively. Something hit the metal roofing.

Trouble had come home.

CHAPTER 11

"WHAT WAS THAT?" Tanya jumped to her feet and ran to the window. She watched as Lucas crouched down low, slipped behind a building and headed over to the far side of the property. She glanced around, trying to see what she'd heard and where'd it had come from. There was a flash of light on top of the hill. "I think somebody just shot at your dog pen," she cried out.

Meg stared at her. "What?"

Top Hat struggled to his feet and eased his way over to her, a low growl escaping. He stared out the glass doors, which offered him visibility from his height.

Tanya bent down beside him. "It's okay, boy. You're not going back there."

Top Hat turned to look her in the eyes. She smiled, not seeing any aggression in him. She reached up and scratched him under the chin and on the back of the head. "But you're injured and in pain. Stay put."

Just as she said that, there was another shot. She cried out, and Top Hat, instead of skulking, bristled.

He barked at the glass door. She looked at Meg. "What should we do?"

"I'd probably let him out," Meg said. "Lucas would know how to get him under control."

Tanya pulled out her phone and called Lucas. "Top Hat

wants to join you. Were those shots fired?"

"Yes," he said. "But I don't want the dog out here because he could get shot again."

"It will get scary in here," she said, "because he has absolutely no intention of sticking around if he can get outside. His barking will wake up the kids."

"Fine. Open the door. I'll call him to me."

"Will do," she said. She walked over to Top Hat and opened the door.

Top Hat bolted outside. There was a whistle, and Top Hat raced for it.

Another shot was fired and missed Top Hat.

Tanya swore and turned to find Meg calling the police.

That was exactly what needed to happen. "Tell him to contact the detective in charge of the dogfighting raids."

Meg filled in the police dispatcher and told them to send someone quickly. Tanya darted around the house, looking through windows. Two children were in this house, and, although they slept, she didn't know for how long. Soon. through a window, she saw another glint coming around the property. She texted Lucas, letting him know what was happening.

The response was instant. **I see it.** It was followed by an order. **Stay inside.**

She snorted, then heard a gun cocking and turned to Meg, surprised. "Do you have another one?"

Meg laughed. "Anybody in the country has at least two," she said. She walked over to a gun cabinet and pulled out a second shotgun, then locked it back up.

Tanya hadn't fired a gun in a long time. Lucas had taught her. He'd said it was better to know how to use a gun and not need it than to have one and not know how to use it.

At the time she'd laughed, but he had been insistent that she learn to load and how to shoot. She was not into target practice because it was loud. But, right now, she was damn grateful to have this gun in her hand.

She texted Lucas. **Both of us holding loaded shotguns.**

There was no answer, but she figured he'd gotten the message. She turned toward Meg, who was at the back door talking on the phone. She went to her side. "What's going on?"

"Nathan's pulling all the dogs inside."

"Good. But that won't help get these guys."

"I know."

Another shot was fired outside, and it slammed into the house. Meg raced to where the boys were sleeping. They were fine.

The master bedroom was a little higher because it was a split-level house. Tanya eased over to look out the window. She caught sight of Lucas on the left side of the property, sneaking around the top of the hill with Top Hat at his side. She wanted to scream at him to get out of sight, but he was too far away, and she didn't want to draw any attention to him. But her breath caught in her throat as she spotted another flash from the morning sun reflecting off a rifle as it was leveled in Lucas's direction.

She shoved open a window and popped out her shotgun. "Don't you dare."

The rifle turned toward her. She fired the double-barrel weapon without a thought. She watched as dirt kicked up in front of the rifle, and then no one was there. She didn't know if she'd hit anyone. She didn't give a damn. They were trying to kill Lucas and Top Hat. This was private property.

She could feel a rage, an old rage she'd tamped down for a long time. It had burst free with Claire and Alice. Right now she wanted a target for all that pent-up rage.

She headed back to the kitchen, popped two more shells out of the box on the counter and reloaded her shotgun, then stuffed six more shells into her pockets.

She looked up to see Meg staring at her—her face white and her eyes dark. She shook her head. "So far everybody's fine, but I was making sure nobody got a shot off at Lucas or Nathan."

Meg nodded. "Thank you."

Tanya gave her a grim smile. "We're in this together," she said. "I'll be damned if those assholes are the last ones standing."

LUCAS COULDN'T BELIEVE she was armed and ready. Once she'd fired her shot, he'd already made his way around to the house, and, as he came around a side building, somebody tried to lift a weapon, which Lucas yanked from his hand. "Do you really want to take that chance?"

The man swore softly. "No, I'm done," he whispered through gritted teeth, falling to the ground. "She got my hand. I'll be lucky if I have the use of it again."

"I won't feel one damn bit sorry for you either," Lucas said, bending down to check out the hand. "Not bad for one shot. Phone, wallet. Now."

The injured man slowly reached into his pocket and pulled out his phone and wallet. He handed them over.

"Cops are on the way," Lucas said. "Either you can sit here and bleed to death or you can make your way down the driveway, and, with any luck, you'll be picked up by the cops first."

The guy only moaned.

"You better get some pressure on that fast." He ripped the guy's T-shirt and bound the wound. "I'm not happy you are here," he said. "And, if you think we aren't shooting the rest of your buddies, you're wrong. *Dead* wrong."

"I warned Joe last night that you were not somebody to mess with," the man said. "My name is Jake. If I don't make it, make sure somebody tells my wife."

"Somebody will tell your wife all right," Lucas said. "Is that really how you want her to find out?"

He shook his head. "No, she told me to get out of the business a long time ago. But I wouldn't listen."

"And why is that?" Lucas asked. "Because you know this will just get uglier."

Jake shrugged. "I've known these guys since high school. I'm the lightweight. They will expect me to be the first one taken out." He swore as he looked at his hand and saw the blood already seeping through the cloth. "I feel like this is pretty major."

"Yep," Lucas said. He already had his phone out, contacting Detective Madison. "I've got one down, with major bleeding."

The detective swore into the phone. "You've got a tactical team coming at you. How bad is it?"

"There's at least four of them." He looked at the Jake, whose gaze shifted sideways. "Or at least twice that."

Jake gave a half nod. "Jake is nodding, which means we got one down and seven to go. But I got my sister, two little boys, my brother-in-law, Tanya and a lot of innocent animals on this property. You know I won't let this go down without a fight."

"We're on the way," the detective said. "Try to stay down until we get there."

"Bring some body bags with you then." Lucas ended the call. "Start walking. If you're lucky, your own buddies won't pop you before you get to the end of the drive."

Jake shot him a look. "Don't underestimate them. Most are ex-military, with three draft dodgers from Idaho."

"Great," Lucas said. "I hope I meet them face-to-face. I don't have much use for dogfighting monsters or deserters."

"Give me a hand up?" Jake asked.

Lucas stretched a hand down, helping Jake to his feet, pointing him in the direction of the driveway. "Go."

He didn't give Jake a chance to argue, he turned and disappeared with Top Hat at his side. **One down, seven to go.** He sent that info to his brother-in-law with a warning. **Watch your back.**

He thought he saw a flash off a rifle. That was the problem with a handgun versus a rifle. Reflections from a handgun barrel were easy to hide but reflections from a rifle barrel, not so much. Keeping to the trees, he snuck up and circled around so he was slightly higher. He crouched down to the ground, Top Hat at his side, his growl low. Lucas reached out a hand to still him. "Easy, boy. We can't let them know we're here."

The two watched intently, Lucas scanning the area, and finally a shift of movement gave away someone's position on the opposite side of where Lucas was. He noted the position and spotted the metal blinking in the light. There were *two* men.

Suddenly gunfire erupted on the far side of the property, the sounds distant but disruptive. Using the disturbance, the two men stood and started shooting in his direction. Lucas let out one warning shot, and, as they fired a second time, he took them both out.

"Well, that's three," Lucas said and slipped down the hillside to where the two men lay dead.

He relieved them of their weapons and left them lying where they were.

He sent Nathan a text. **Two down.**

He replied, **Two here too.**

Lucas sent back **One walking driveway, bleeding wrist. Leaves three.**

Another shot was fired from the house, and a man toppled from a tree down to the property.

He sent Nathan another text. **Another one down. Two more to go.**

He crouched down low, waiting in the stillness—definitely a game of patience. He knew the cops would be here soon, and they would need meat wagons for the bodies.

With six down, two left, Lucas knew one of them would be the asshole Joe from the restaurant last night. Lucas skulked around the house to see one man slinking to the front, peering in through the window. As soon as he felt his presence, he spun around, aiming his gun at Lucas, but Lucas already had a rifle on him.

"Drop it," Lucas said in a low, menacing tone. "I'm not giving you the benefit of the doubt. You drop that right now, or I will kill you."

The man lowered his weapon.

Lucas knocked him under the chin with the butt of his rifle, stunning him, and the guy dropped to the ground. Bending down, Lucas pulled out his victim's phone and wallet. He walked over to the basket of crap Meg had on the

veranda and pulled out strips of old shirts and used that to
tie him up. He rolled the man over, gave him a nudge and
said, "Joe's the last one, isn't he?"

"For the moment, yes."

"He chose the wrong person to bring the war home to.
This is what I do for a living," Lucas said. "And I'm more
than happy to take Joe out." He left the man trussed up in
the front yard for the police to find. Seven down, one bastard
to go.

He took off around the house. Top Hat kept up with
him. He zigzagged around the trees and stopped in his tracks
when he heard a voice behind him.

"Think you're so goddamn smart, don't you? Right now,
you don't have a hope in hell," Joe said. And he cocked his
rifle.

Top Hat exploded with snarling and barking and baring
his teeth. Lucas dropped to a crouch, spun and took aim.
Only Joe was already down with Top Hat at his throat.

Lucas called off Top Hat. But he wasn't listening to the
order. "Stop," Lucas ordered, louder this time. "Top Hat,
guard."

Top Hat growled and changed his grip to Joe's shoulder
and clamped down tight and hard.

Joe screamed.

Lucas sighed. "Joe, Joe, Joe. Stop your whining. Did you
really think you would get away with this?"

"Call him off me," Joe screamed again.

Lucas looked at Top Hat and with a hand command, he
had Top Hat backing off.

The shepherd sauntered beside Lucas unwillingly,
whimpering.

Lucas rubbed his head. "Good boy," he said. "Good

boy."

Joe reared up, pulling a knife from his belt and tried to stab Top Hat. Lucas didn't waste any time. He fired. And took out Joe's knife arm at the shoulder joint. The same place Top Hat had bit him. The same place where Top Hat had been shot.

Joe collapsed, screaming in agony.

Lucas smiled. Eight shitheads taken out. "Now we're even, you asshole."

CHAPTER 12

TANYA RACED OUTSIDE, having seen Lucas take down a man who looked like Joe.

Lucas raised his head with his rifle, and she stopped abruptly, saying, "It's me."

He lowered his gun and said, "I could have shot you, Tanya. Don't rush up to a guy holding a gun, when he's not sure he's taken out the last of the bad guys."

"I should have let you know I was coming," she admitted. "I'm sorry." She approached a little more cautiously. "That's the asshole from the restaurant, isn't it?"

"It so is." In the distance, they heard sirens approaching.

"Good timing on their part," she said drily. "Now they get to ride into the rescue with everything already taken care of."

"But they get to mop up the mess," Lucas said cheerfully. He straightened up as Joe tried to roll over, but he dropped down hard on his back. "Stay there," Lucas ordered, "or my next bullet will be between your eyes."

Four cop cars came up the driveway to Meg's house. Lucas glanced at Tanya. "Everybody okay inside?"

She nodded. "And, believe it or not, the boys are still asleep."

He chuckled. "At that age, I slept through bombs too. What about Nathan and Meg?"

"I don't know," she said worriedly, turning to look toward the pens. "I came out here, and Meg was heading to the pens."

"We'll check on them in a second, as soon as I know this guy's not going anywhere."

The cops swarmed around them. Lucas held up his hands, his weapon on the ground. Tanya lay hers down on the ground and held up her hands as well.

One of the officers got out of his vehicle. "Are you Lucas?" he asked.

"I am," he said. "I want to make sure this asshole doesn't get loose. He's one of the ringleaders who brought the attack to my sister's place."

Two cops came forward and pulled Joe up and handcuffed him. He screamed, "My shoulder."

"I wouldn't worry about your shoulder," Lucas said. "You had no business coming here. You brought the war to us. So, as far as I'm concerned, everything you get from here on out, you deserve that and so much more."

"If you hadn't stuck your nose in our business …" Joe snapped, his face turning red. "We wouldn't have needed this talk."

The cops stared at Joe like he had sprouted two heads. "The law doesn't work that way," one said.

"He's a suspect in the dogfighting raids," Lucas said. "I've got the rest of Joe's men all over the place here. Most are dead."

Dead? Tanya paled. She wanted to find Meg and Nathan. She turned and walked away from the chaos and headed for the pens. Halfway there she saw Meg and Nathan walking to the house. Meg took one look at her. "Is it over?"

Tanya nodded. "It is. They will start collecting the bodies. The boys are still asleep."

"Thank God for that," Nathan said. "Please tell me that you at least checked that they were still breathing."

Tanya smiled. "I did, indeed."

With the two heading inside and looking no worse for wear, Tanya headed back toward Lucas. The men looked up as she approached. Only two cops were left in front, and they were talking on their phones. Lucas sat on the front step.

She sat beside him. "Nathan and Meg are fine and are going inside to the boys," she said.

"Good," he said and wrapped an arm around her shoulders and pulled her against his body.

"Where's Top Hat?"

He nodded toward his truck, then he kissed the top of her head softly and said, "You did real good out there. Thanks for having my six."

"Wouldn't it be nice if I didn't have to remember all your lessons?" she asked with a smirk. "It's generally a quiet community, and we don't need to defend ourselves against asshats like these guys."

"Hopefully this will be the end of it."

One of the cops finished his phone call, walked over and said, "So, you guys want to fill us in on what the hell happened up here?" He held up his phone and said, "I'll record this."

Lucas nodded. "Record away." He started at the beginning with Top Hat and told the whole story.

Tanya nodded. "Speaking of Top Hat, I'll go check on him." She had a way to go to be completely comfortable with this dog, but he'd been through so much—and so had she—that she couldn't help but feel an affinity for him. The rescue center had said he was aggressive, but she hadn't seen any sign of it—at least not directed at her.

She walked to Lucas's truck. Sure enough, Top Hat was on the back seat. His eyes were wide, and his fur was sticking up. When he saw her, he whined.

She smiled. "Hey, Top Hat. It's been a tough day. It'll get much better now though."

Lucas walked over to her. He wrapped his hand around the leash and urged Top Hat out of the truck. "This guy needs to go to the bathroom."

He walked him over to a grassy spot to allow Top Hat to relieve himself. As soon as he was done, Top Hat walked a few steps to a puddle and had a drink.

"He's doing much better," Tanya said.

"But still has a way to go."

"When did you put him in the truck?" she asked.

"When you went looking for Meg and Nathan. I needed him to calm down, so I put him in the truck for his safety."

She nodded. "That was smart."

"That's why Joe over there was screaming about his shoulder. I shot him, hitting the same place Top Hat had latched onto and wouldn't let go."

"Also smart," she said. "Joe's nothing but scum. He deserves to be ripped to pieces by a dog."

After that, the cops had a lot of questions for her. She did her best to answer everything. She also told them about Claire's death, then Alice's accident and her firing.

"Do you really think they are connected?" a cop asked.

"Maybe," she said. "You guys should know more than we do. There's a lot we don't know."

"And none of these guys were kind enough to enlighten us before they were eliminated. Joe and Jake aren't talking," Lucas added.

Tanya moved in closer. Lucas wrapped his arms around her, holding her tight.

The cop looked up from his note taking. "Do you know of anybody at your previous company who would be connected to this ring?"

"No," she said. "But that doesn't mean someone—Alice possibly—wasn't handling one of the group's accounts. She handled very different accounts than I did so it's possible."

"Maybe," the cop said, but he didn't look convinced. She just wanted it all to go away.

"Too bad we can't ask Alice questions," she said suddenly. As much as she wanted this to go away, Alice was a constant reminder. "She's still not conscious."

"She was the victim of the hit-and-run, correct?"

Tanya nodded.

The cop thanked her for her statement and walked off, still writing down notes.

Lucas snapped a picture of Joe, then Jake. He nodded toward the bodies being carted over to the vans for transport and asked the technicians to open the body bags to snap pics of their faces too, avoiding anything gruesome. He needed his own record as they still didn't know which cops were involved in this fiasco.

Tanya waited with Top Hat, who now rested on the grass.

Meg and Nathan stepped out on the porch to give their statements.

"So, can we leave?" Tanya asked.

"There'll be many more hours of evidence gathering," Lucas said.

They headed over to Meg and Nathan after the police walked away from them.

"Not exactly the calm morning we had expected, is it?"

Meg snorted. "No, but sometimes you have to stand up for what is right. Coffee's fresh if you want a cup."

Lucas walked inside and was soon back with two cups. "Listen, Meg, Nathan. I'm sorry. I didn't mean for this to come to your front door."

"We know," Nathan said. "Hopefully it's over."

"True enough," Lucas said. "Maybe they will find a connection with Claire's death, Alice's accident and Tanya's firing."

"Oh," Meg said. "Seriously?"

Nathan stared in disbelief. "Is that what they're thinking?"

"We don't know all the details, but they are leaning in that direction. Tanya's situation will be harder to prove. It seems, over the last couple days, we took out of commission quite a few of the men involved in the local dogfighting rings. Several are dead. The few remaining will be charged and won't be seeing daylight anytime soon."

"The question is whether they have the boss or the ringleaders of this ring," Meg said. "They also caught a lot of people in Red Deer, right?"

"Yes," Lucas said with a hard nod. "And the authorities are still working on it."

"I don't think any of the men involved have been as violent as Joe and the others here though," Tanya said. "Apparently we set off a domino effect."

"That's because of us," Lucas said. "More specifically me. Maybe you should go home and stay there where you're safe."

"Now you're telling me to stay home where it's safe?" she asked in outrage. "I don't know. I'd say, if there is a ringleader still out there, I'm not safe away from you. Whether you like it or not, I am involved."

Nathan said, "I told everything I know to the cops, and they collected all the cell phones from these eight men. It will take the police time to sift through that, but we have to trust they have this well in hand."

"They do," Lucas said. "They were already sorting through Joe's buddies' phones and comparing details."

LUCAS STOOD, NODDED to the two cops he'd spoken to earlier.

"We could use you downtown. We have a few more questions."

"I can do that," he said. He glanced back at the others. "Can everyone else stay here?"

The cops nodded. "We have a conference with some of our cohorts in Red Deer. We've got the net widening even as we speak. We found several other suspects in the contacts list in the phones. We have teams heading out to round up more people. This is one of the biggest cases we've ever had, and, hopefully, by the end of the day, we'll have everybody."

Lucas smiled. "Now that would be a good thing."

"Meet you downtown in thirty minutes?" the cop asked, checking his watch.

Lucas nodded. "Sure. Tanya and I are gonna grab a bite to eat, and we'll head over afterward. She stays with me."

The officers nodded. "Want us to drive you?"

Lucas shook his head. "No, I'll take my own wheels. Thanks. See you there."

They shook hands and walked away. Lucas turned back

to Tanya, Meg and Nathan and rolled his eyes. Meg and Nathan headed inside while Lucas pulled out his phone.

He hated the suspicion, but it was always there in the back of his head. He contacted Detective Madison in Red Deer. "I've already had to deal with one cop on the wrong side of this case. Now I'm a little hesitant about the two just here asking me to go down to the station. They even offered to drive me there."

"What were their names?" Detective Madison asked.

Lucas gave the names and the license plate of the cruiser as it pulled away. "They're leaving now."

"Hang on. I'll call the station and see who is asking for you to go in. I'll call you back."

The call ended, and Lucas pocketed his phone. Turning to Tanya, he said, "We'll grab a bite to eat and head to the station, if it's cleared by Madison."

"Do we have to go?"

"Depends if it's a legal and official request," he said. "In which case, not going could lead to trouble." He eyed her. "I was actually thinking I should follow them and see if I can push them into doing something that would show if they're involved. One cop who showed up at Andy's place is definitely no good, so what's the chance he's the only one that is?"

"There will be more," she said. "Rarely is it just one. They come in pairs."

He chuckled. "And why is that?"

"Because they often work as partners, and it's pretty hard to pull something like that on your partner."

"Good point," Lucas said. "If I get to the station, and they're not there, and nobody has questions for me, then I'll leave my name and number, and they can call me back in again."

She nodded. "I'm starving. Let's get food."

Top Hat decided to chime in and let out a bark. He was trying to jump up in the truck.

"You're too injured, buddy. You should stay behind." But Top Hat wasn't having anything to do with that.

As soon as Lucas opened the driver's side door to get in, Top Hat hopped up. And when Lucas tried to get him to come back out again, Top Hat jumped over the seat onto the back bench.

Tanya laughed. "I think he has made up his mind. The whole family is going."

Lucas shook his head but grinned, hopped in the truck, more pleased than he expected at her wording.

As soon as he turned on the engine, he said, "Send Meg a text, won't you? Tell her what we're doing, so she doesn't worry."

"I can do that," Tanya said, pulling out her phone.

As they drove away, he asked, "Did you mean it?"

"Did I mean what?" she asked, looking up at him.

"*Family*," he said, "That's what you said. The whole *family* was going with me."

"Oh." She stared at him for a moment. "Of course I meant it."

"Well, *family* is a touchy topic for you," he said.

"Always has been, I guess," she said. "I don't know if I'll enjoy the process of working my way through the hows and the whys, but I am willing to try."

"Try what?" he asked, needing clarity.

"To see why it is I am so against motherhood and deal with these roadblocks. And, once we're done with the cops, maybe we could stop in at my mom's?"

"We can do that," he said. As they drove along, he asked, "Does this mean we're not broken up?"

She laughed. "Honestly, we never were broken up, were we?"

He half grinned at her. "I was just giving you space. Time and space to figure out what you wanted."

"Thank you for that," she said. "I never stopped loving you."

"Ditto," he said gently. "But it's been very lonely. I do still want a family too, but we'll have to work out that issue."

"I might not be able to have any," she warned.

"You've said that many times."

"I'm hoping, when I get to that point, I'll be more than happy to have children, but, if not, I don't know."

"But you said you are willing to explore that?" He took his eyes off the road and looked at her. "Did you mean it?"

She nodded solemnly. "I really want to. With you."

He knew she'd make a fantastic mom. But she had so much baggage from her childhood and from her own mom. A lot of work needed to be done. "Let's take one day at a time and see how we do," he said.

"I can do that," she said in a soft voice. "And thanks for waiting."

He pulled into a local burger joint that had an all day breakfast menu, and they exited together with Top Hat following enthusiastically, his nose sniffing the air. Lucas wrapped his hand around the leash and let Tanya lead the way. The waitress didn't even bat an eye when Top Hat entered with them. They sat at a booth and Top Hat lay under the table.

The waitress brought over glasses of water and menus.

Lucas already knew what he wanted. "Can we order

right away?" he asked.

"Sure," she replied and took out a notepad.

"Double burger, everything on it, fries on the side, chocolate shake. Four hamburger patties, nothing on them, no bun."

She nodded, turned to look at Tanya. "*Uhm*, I'll have a single burger, with cheese, ketchup and mayo, strawberry milkshake, please."

"No side?" the waitress asked.

Tanya shook her head. "No, thanks."

When the waitress left, they each leaned back in their seats and let out deep sighs. It felt like the first chance they'd had to relax and breathe since all this started.

Before they knew it, their food was placed on the table. Lucas sliced up the patties for Top Hat and set the plate at his feet. Top Hat ate as they did, fast and efficiently. Nobody was talking, the food was that good.

Lucas got one text toward the end of dinner from Detective Madison, saying he hadn't tracked down the officers, so please show up at the station and let him know once Lucas signed in at reception.

They arrived at the station a short time later. Lucas said, "Do you want to stay here until I check this out?"

"I'll stay with Top Hat," she said. "Text me if we are supposed to be in there answering questions."

He nodded and headed into the station.

CHAPTER 13

TANYA SAT IN the passenger seat of Lucas's truck and waited. Top Hat crashed on the backseat. Meg sent a text acknowledging she received Tanya's earlier text. Other than that, Tanya sat quietly, contemplating how much her life had changed. She really did want to go see her mother, to find out if it felt any differently now. She felt ashamed for walking away for so long. Especially when it came to her brothers. Not so much about her mother though. Walking away was one thing—staying away was something else altogether.

Sure, it had not been an easy childhood for Tanya, and she had felt justified leaving to make her own life, but sometimes one needed to have things highlighted and behaviors acknowledged in order to change them.

She also had to go back to work tomorrow, and that was a bit of a challenge too. She hated her current job, but there wasn't much chance of changing it right now. She still had rent to pay, so she would work tomorrow morning regardless.

As she sat there, she remembered her old company and the pain of being fired. Such a humbling experience. Especially for embezzlement. Which she'd finally been cleared of, but the stigma had stayed. She pulled out her phone and opened an internet page. She typed her former boss's name into her phone to see if she could find more details about his family.

When the door opened suddenly, she had been concentrating so hard, reading various hits from her search that she was startled. She gasped as Lucas hopped back in the truck. When she caught her breath, she asked, "So?"

"There might be more questions, but they don't have anything right now. It's chaotic in there. Head to your mother's?"

"I was wondering something while you were inside. I don't suppose any of the bad guys are related to my old boss?"

"Related in what way?"

"Any way," she said with a laugh. "Just wondering if he got rid of me at someone else's request. You know? A reason to explain why my world blew up. Everyone is wondering that, but what about proof?"

"Let the cops do their investigation first. Where is your mother living these days?"

As soon as Lucas pulled out of the parking lot, Tanya said, "Still in the same place."

"I remember where that is," he said.

"How could you? That was a while ago."

"Sure, but we drove past it a couple times. Even though you always wanted to disconnect that tie, you haven't been able to. That's what family is all about," he said with a smirk.

"It's not fair though," she said. "We should be allowed to disconnect at times."

"In some cases, people do. But you have a lot of time, energy and love invested in that family."

"And yet, I tried so hard to walk away."

"And maybe you should look at *why*."

"Because I'd had enough," she said. "It was basically slavery. And I'm sure a lot of kids feel that way when they're growing up. I had to get away in order to change the status quo."

"And you did," he said. "Nobody's judging you for that."

"No?" she cried out. "I'm judging myself. I feel like I let them all down. I should have stayed. I should have helped them because Mom was such a terrible mother. I feel like, by walking away, I basically deserted them too."

"But you waited until she came back out of rehab and waited until she was much more stable before you walked away, so you gave all of them the best chance possible."

"I don't think it matters," Tanya said. "I knew in my heart she wouldn't be a good mom."

"Do you blame your sisters for walking away?"

She looked at him, startled. "Of course not. They did what they needed to do. Two left to go to college and get an education, the other two left to find good jobs."

He looked at her and smiled. "So why is it that they're okay to walk away, but you aren't?"

"Because I was the surrogate mother," she stated bluntly. "They never were."

"But they could have been, right? They could have stepped up and taken your place so you could leave. They didn't. They left because they were looking after themselves."

"I urged them to leave," she said. "I knew they had no future if they stayed there."

"You got two out. The next two were well on their way, and the twins were coming up behind. How can you still blame yourself for not sticking around?"

"An oversize sense of guilt I guess," she said. "Not to

mention the bonds you form when you're growing up. It still feels like I could have done more for them all."

"Sometimes you have to acknowledge that you've done what you could, and, for your own sake, for your own sanity, you have to walk away. I don't know what you were like when you first left, but I can't imagine it was an easy decision."

"I was desperate," she said. "I hadn't slept in a long time. I'd lost so much weight that people were starting to notice."

"Exactly," he said quietly. "You might hate that you weren't strong enough to stick around, but the bottom line is, you did what you could. You were still a child. Your own health suffered, and your mother didn't care."

"I don't know what my mother felt," she said in frustration. "That's one of the biggest things about living with a drug addict. They say anything to get what they want, and you can never really believe anything that comes out of their mouth." Just then she motioned and said, "Take a left coming up."

He took the next left turn. "Maybe I don't remember the way," he said. "I don't recognize the area."

"It's been a while since we drove past."

He pulled off to the side of the road. "It's that one up ahead, isn't it?"

She leaned forward. "Yes. Two houses up. The lawn is still not mowed. The front still needs a paint job, and the wood around the windows is peeling. I guess the twins aren't doing anything to keep up the house."

"They're fourteen," Lucas said gently. "The only things they give a damn about are sports, girls and computer games."

She chuckled. "Isn't that the truth?"

He nodded. "You want to go see her, or is this enough?"

"I think I need to see her." Resolutely she pushed open the door and hopped out. And when he didn't move, she looked at him through the open doorway. "Do you want to come or stay here and wait?"

"I'll bring Top Hat out so he can walk around and stretch out a bit. Then I'll join you."

She gave him a strange look. "Meaning that, if I don't feel like it's going okay, if I do feel like going, and I need help, you'll come and bail me out?"

"Meaning, I'll let Top Hat have a walk around because it's good for him, and, in the meantime, you make a decision on what you'll do," he said gently. "Don't make this heavier than it needs to be. Go say hi or don't."

She nodded, turned and walked away.

HE HATED TO see how much this tormented her. But there was nothing easy about her family. She'd had no child-hood—nobody would judge her for it except herself. And, of course, that was always the worst. He knew he was the hardest on himself as well.

But her mother's failing health brought a lot to the forefront. He admitted he was surprised at Tanya's softening stance on family. When he'd come up for Top Hat, he had not expected to be rekindling this relationship. Or maybe he should have because, always in the back of his mind, he hadn't considered himself free; he'd always considered himself as partnered with her. He'd spoken the truth about giving her space.

Even though they'd clearly broken up, and he knew it

was foolish to keep holding on, it had seemed like they hadn't completed their business. He still loved her, always had.

He gently helped Top Hat get out and walked him down the sidewalk to loosen up his joints. His shoulder was stiff, but he was moving pretty good. He had done a lot this morning and that would impact his healing, set him back a bit. Lucas reached down and gently scratched him under the neck and shoulder.

He took a pic of Top Hat and sent it to the vet. **He's up and moving, looking good.**

The text was answered immediately with several happy emojis.

He chuckled, tucked his phone back in his pocket and headed down the street to Tanya's mother's house. The fact that she still had possession of the house was amazing. Either there was no mortgage on it or the bank hadn't found a way to get rid of her. Because he knew, chances were pretty strong she was not making regular payments.

He hadn't had the experience Tanya had, and yet, every time he had driven by this place, he got bad vibes. By the time he got to the front door, Top Hat was moving in a good rhythm. The shoulder was still sore, as he favored it slightly, but he walked in a much more relaxed manner. He seemed happy to be out. Lucas knocked on the door and told Top Hat to relax and sit.

The door was opened by a young man who looked at Lucas and then at the dog, his eyebrows rising. "So you're her boyfriend?"

He nodded. "I am. Is she still here?"

"Yeah, she is. Surprisingly." He opened the door wider and said, "You might as well come in." He looked at Top

Hat. "What's wrong with him?"

"He was shot," Lucas said smoothly and stepped inside. He had to admit, if a young woman had been at the door, he probably wouldn't have said it so bluntly, but, because it was a guy, he thoroughly expected the reaction he got.

"Shot?" Instantly the dog became a hit. He stuck out his hand. "I'm Tom, Tanya's brother."

Lucas shook his hand and said, "I'm Lucas. This is Top Hat."

The kid crouched in front of Top Hat. The dog looked at him warily. "Is he dangerous?" Tom asked.

His twin came over to join them, probably at the word *shot*. He introduced himself as Tennessee and then crouched in front of the dog. "Is he badly hurt?"

"The vets stitched him up, and he's moving around now."

"Why did he get shot?"

"Because a dogfighting ring wanted him for their fights, and he wasn't cooperating."

The boys were completely fascinated. "Are you a cop?"

"No," he said. "Ex-military."

Both boys gaped at him with a touch of awe. Lucas chuckled. "So, where's your sister?"

"She's in the kitchen. Come on." The boys led him there.

As soon as they saw their mother, one of them piped up, "Mom, I'm hungry."

The other one said, "Lucas and Top Hat are here."

Lucas stepped into the kitchen to see the two women at either side of a table with odd looks on their faces as they turned to look at him. "I hope I'm not intruding," he said quietly.

Tanya hopped to her feet. "Of course not." She walked over to him, smiled and said, "Let me introduce you to my mother."

He stepped forward and reached out a hand to shake the woman's hand. She didn't seem to know what to do with his but managed to shake it. She nodded when he introduced himself and pointed to Top Hat. "I hope it's all right he came in."

She stared at the dog, but he could see she was either drugged out because of the pain or drugged out from something else because almost nothing made an impression on her.

In a low voice, Tanya said, "I think my presence shocked her."

"I'm sure it did," he said. "Are you staying or ..." He let his words hang.

Her mother hopped to her feet and said, "No, she's leaving. I don't know why she stopped by in the first place." She did sound bewildered.

"It's to be expected," Lucas said quietly. "She just found out about your illness. It's easy to forget about all the things we don't want to deal with until we realize somebody might not be here later on."

"There's nothing for us to deal with," her mother said sharply. "We dealt with it a long time ago."

"Did we?" Tanya asked.

"Yes," her mother said bitterly. "The day you walked."

"What about every day that you walked out the eighteen years before that?" Tanya asked.

Her mother just glared at her. "I was sick. You know that."

"You were sick on drugs and alcohol, yes," Tanya said.

"And turning tricks at every corner."

Her mother gasped and turned to look at the boys. The boys were staring with avid interest.

"Don't tell me that they haven't a clue," Tanya said.

Her mother's face flushed, and her bottom lip trembled.

Tanya asked, "What have you been doing to support everyone these last few years?"

"I work at Walmart," her mother said. "Not that you care."

"I do care," Tanya said. "When did this start?"

"After you walked."

"So maybe it was a good thing I did leave," Tanya said. "If I had stayed, you would have been in the same damn cycle as before. I'm not sure rehab would have done any good."

Her mother sat down slowly. "Well, it did. I managed to stay off drugs. The alcohol, well, I have a little bit now and again but not too much," she said, her gaze once again darting to the boys.

"If they have any idea of what you've been through," Lucas said, "I wouldn't think hiding the truth is any help."

She turned her gaze on him and glared. "You don't know anything about it."

"Only what Tanya has told me," he said. "I've certainly heard lots though."

"She's been gone for a long time," her mother said. "So it doesn't really matter."

"I'm also sorry about that," Tanya said abruptly. "You turned me into a mother and a caregiver instead of allowing me to have a childhood. I had to leave to get an education and to find my own way. Maybe, like I said, it was the best thing. I'm glad you straightened up. I'm glad you raised these boys."

"I lost the other girls too," her mom said with a note of bitterness. "Nobody was there to help me."

"We all helped you as much as we could, but we had to get out to save ourselves."

Her mother glared at her. "I don't know what you're talking about," she said defensively.

"You were trying to get me to turn tricks for you, *Mom*. Don't think I don't remember that," she said. "The girls had to take off to college as soon as they could, to get away too, before you brought men to them, giving them no choice."

The brothers left the kitchen—whether they had heard enough or didn't even notice, they both had peanut butter sandwiches in their hands and were talking about a video game.

Tanya's mom sagged back. "I try not to bring all the details up with the boys."

"Ignorance is bliss when you have that option," Tanya said. "I didn't have that option, so you can be as mad as you want, but I needed to leave. But I am sorry I left as completely as I did because I think it hurt everybody."

"We were fine without you," her mother said in a harsh tone. "So you can just take off now too."

Tanya sighed. "You know what? You're probably right. I don't know why I was even interested in seeing you. I'm sorry about your health issues. If there's anything you need, call. I'm not doing so great myself right now." She turned and headed for the front door, and Lucas followed her.

She stopped at the living room where the boys were. "If you guys need anything, give me a shout."

They didn't even raise their heads to acknowledge her. She sighed and walked out.

Lucas, on the other hand, pulled two cards from his pocket and dropped them on the floor in front of the boys. "If you guys get into trouble, get in touch."

They looked at the cards, looked at him and said, "Cool."

He walked out.

Tanya stood on the front step, taking deep breaths.

He couldn't blame her. There wasn't an easy answer. "I'm sorry," he said.

"What did I expect?" she asked. "It's not like there's any open arms for me."

"No, but like you said, you've been gone a long time, so it's hard to say exactly how anybody feels anymore, right?"

She nodded and walked down the stairs. "It's still harsh," she said.

"Just give it some time. Facing your mother wouldn't be easy. You knew that before going in there." He patted her shoulder, watching her eyes.

Just then a cop car drove by. She looked at it and said, "Will I always wonder if the cops I see are involved in the dogfighting ring?"

"I don't know," he said, his own gaze studying the vehicle. "It's quite possible. But that's not one of the known men involved." He walked back to the truck and helped Top Hat up into the back seat.

"The dog is doing much better," she said.

"He is, indeed." Inside the truck, they sat and looked at each other. "Now where?"

She smiled. "Good question. Are we going back to your sister's?"

He pulled out his phone and called Meg. "How's everything there?" he asked.

"We're exhausted, but the place is empty now. The boys are up, and I just finished making pancakes," she said with a laugh. "From chaos to routine—life with children."

"We just visited with Tanya's mother, and we're at loose ends."

"Come on back here then," she said. "You don't have to stay away. Besides, I think it would be good if Top Hat had a chance to get accustomed to being here since you'll be around a lot more now. We'll be a second home for him, so to speak. Presuming you are keeping him, right?"

"Right," he said, realizing he had lots of decisions to make. The bottom line was, he didn't want to lose Top Hat or Tanya. He glanced at Tanya to see her watching him and realized she could probably hear Meg. "We'll be there in a bit. Do you want me to pick up anything?"

"See? Right back to normalcy," Meg said. "We'll have steaks on the barbecue for dinner in a couple hours. Pick up stuff for Caesar salad, some soft drinks, paper towels and dessert. Something with chocolate."

"Will do." He ended the call. "She wants us to pick up a few things at the grocery store."

Tanya nodded but didn't say anything.

As he went to turn on the engine, he looked at her. "Do you need to go home? Do you have things you should do?"

She shook her head. "No. I'm okay. It's just strange. I have to go back to work tomorrow, and it'll feel like a completely different world again."

"True."

"We could go to the park with Top Hat. I'm sure he'd like to relax outside for a bit."

They stopped at a corner store and grabbed bottles of water and a snack for Top Hat, then headed to a small park, where Lucas helped Top Hat out of the truck and let him wander around the park, his leash dragging behind him.

Lucas smiled at Tanya's happy face. "This is how I remember you. Always smiling."

"I haven't really had a lot to smile about lately," she said.

"I think we have to make reasons to smile. Make reasons to be happy. We can't always expect others or life to give us what we need."

"Since when did you become so philosophical?" she asked.

"I don't know," he said, "but it's true."

"Maybe, but it's sad when you see your mother in the condition mine is in."

"Don't worry about it. One day at a time, remember?"

"I thought that was for our relationship," she said, chuckling.

"I would think it's about everything."

They sat there for a long moment until finally she said, "Let's go get the shopping done, go visit with your sister and enjoy a home-cooked meal, then I can go home and have an early night before returning to work tomorrow."

Lucas stood and called Top Hat. He trotted over and sat down beside Lucas in case there was a treat for good behavior, when something caught his ear. He turned and started to growl. His growl went from a light warning to full-protective mode. Lucas turned and froze.

CHAPTER 14

TANYA'S HEAD POPPED up when she heard Top Hat. She stepped back and turned to look at what was bothering him, then followed Lucas's gaze. He stared at two men in cop uniforms, standing in front of them, guns drawn and pointed at them.

She looked between Lucas and the two men. "You're not even cops. You're just wearing the uniforms."

"What are you talking about?" the men asked.

"You're impersonating cops," she said as she stood far enough behind Lucas that she had her cell phone out and was sending a 9-1-1 text. Then she tried to click on Meg's name.

"Get over here," one of the cop's ordered, waving his gun.

She pocketed her phone and moved forward. "Sure," she said. "Great idea to impersonate cops. But I think that's another charge all on its own."

"Particularly if you took those uniforms off two real cops," Lucas said in a hard tone. "We have to consider whether you killed a cop to get that outfit."

"We didn't kill any cops. These are just uniforms from a cop buddy. You two don't know jack shit," one said. "Come on. Let's get a move on."

"Sure. Where are we going?" Lucas asked, stepping forward.

"Some place where you won't be found. You're the reason all this happened. You're the only one who can testify against us. You and her. She will be taken care of quickly but not until we have taken care of you. She's our bait that will keep you in line," said one guy with a toothy smile.

She stared at him and shuddered. "Seriously? You think that'll work?"

"Yes, it'll work," the guy said. "We're in a public park. Let's go."

She glanced around and saw pathways all throughout the place. But they needed a diversion, something to shift the balance.

Lucas motioned to the side and using his fingers pointed at the path to the trees. Then he held out three fingers ... and dropped one,... then a second one. Finally the third disappeared ...

She bolted.

Gunshots were fired only to be followed by sounds of a fight. She raced down the pathway to the trees, hearing Top Hat bark.

She didn't want to turn around but couldn't help herself. But there was only green—bushes, trees, grass. She could only hope Lucas was either being held at gunpoint or had taken out the enemy. She couldn't hear any footsteps running behind her either. She ran until she was out of breath and then quietly hid in the trees, her fingers busy on her phone. Top Hat was right here with her, his long leash trailing behind them. She grabbed it and took the two of them deeper into the underbrush and made as many phone calls as she could.

She wrapped her arms around the dog who stood, his

gaze forward, locked on the woods outside of where she'd hidden. And she realized she should have hidden someplace where she could have seen around her, instead of being blocked out like she was.

Every sound was magnified; every bird call she heard, to her, was because the bird had taken flight due to danger. She could only trust Top Hat and his early warning system. She waited until his back went up, and he started to growl. She grabbed his jaw and whispered, "*Shh.*"

He went silent, but his gaze never shifted as he stared at something just outside the bush they were hiding in. Damn it. She knew she was about to get caught.

LUCAS DODGED, DROPPED, kicked out and took down the cop holding the gun on him. As he turned to look behind him, he saw Tanya and Top Hat disappear. *Good.* As far as he was concerned that was the best answer. Just as he swiveled back, a boot caught him on the side of his jaw, and he went down. He twisted and snagged the guy midleg, dropped him down and got into an all-out fight, from jaw punches to kicks, then two fast and hard jabs—and the cop in front of him dropped and stayed dropped.

Straddling him and swearing out loud, Lucas tossed his gun to the side, rolled the man over and pulled off his belt and used it to tie him up.

Finally standing and taking deep breaths, trying to calm down, and ease his back knowing he'd pay for this later, he pulled out his phone and sent Tanya a message, saying he had one tied up and to watch out for the second.

Then he heard a scream. He picked up the weapon,

reached down and gave a hard slam to the guy's head to make sure he stayed out and raced in the direction of the scream.

He bolted down the path, running as hard and as fast as he could, when something hard and hot hit him in the shoulder. He hit the ground face-first, planting a big one and crying out at the pain lancing through his shoulder.

He rolled over, took several deep breaths and scrambled to the side to get out of sight, in case the shooter came after him. Hidden in the bushes, he tried to calm his breathing and to slow down the pain. With his hand clasped against his shoulder, he realized the bullet had gone through the muscle on the high side. That was the best result, but it would still leave a hell of a trail.

He listened to see if Tanya made any more noise. She was here somewhere, somewhere in a great deal of pain. And fear. He stood up ever-so-slowly and peered through the bush. There was no sign of anyone. Off to the side a little bit of bush shifted. He remembered Top Hat was out here somewhere. Using a high whistle, he called to the dog. Then shifted position.

If he was being tracked, he needed to make sure he got in the first shot this time. He didn't know that he would get a second chance. That first shot had been a lucky fluke on their part, but it had also been lucky on his part as it hadn't hit anything vital.

From his crouched position, he was momentarily startled by a black nose suddenly poking through the bush. He smiled and whispered, "Hey, Top Hat."

The dog came closer, gently licking his face. "We're a pair, aren't we? Both of us shot in the shoulder. What a nightmare." He gently hugged the dog. Top Hat could smell the wound on him, the blood flowing freely over his fingers. But as best he could, he pressed his shirt up tight against the wound to try and stop the flow. He reached out and scratched Top Hat on the head, hand under the chin. "Where is she?"

Top Hat barked once, then again. When no bullets came in his direction, Lucas slowly straightened, using the tree to get up on his feet again and peered around. He saw nothing. He called out, "Tanya?"

He heard nothing.

He hit Dial on his phone, and her number rang, so he and Top Hat started searching for any sign of her. He didn't like what he found—blood in an area that had been well trampled. Swearing, he realized the other fake cop had taken her.

He crouched down, feeling the pain, accelerating his lightheadedness. He called Detective Madison. When he explained, the detective said, "Don't move. I'll be there soon. I just arrived in town. We've got cops looking."

"They've taken her," he whispered. "I don't know where. Top Hat and I are here in the park. I can see the scene, but there's no sign of her."

"He couldn't have taken her far," the detective said. "We'll see if we can find her before he takes her out of that area."

"Okay," Lucas replied. He ended the call. Trying to keep his head, he shifted backward, looking around for tracks. Top Hat had disappeared on him. He whistled, and Top Hat bolted back toward him, but he didn't come all the way.

He stood and barked, waiting for Lucas to follow him. Lucas took several steps forward, and Top Hat turned to take off in one direction, looking back, as if encouraging him to follow.

Lucas picked up the pace and started to run. Top Hat didn't quit. He kept running, and Lucas wasn't sure how long he could keep going on, but he'd be damned if he'd give up before the dog did, who was running on an injured shoulder. They came to a small parking lot. It was empty, but, in the distance, he could see a black SUV heading down the road. He was too far away to catch a license plate or any sign of the driver.

He called the detective and yelled into the phone, "Black SUV heading south from the park's public parking lot. I've traveled north probably about two miles, but I don't know the name of the street."

"Okay," the detective said. "I've got two locals here with me. We're a couple minutes away."

"If you see a black SUV ripping up the pavement, stop it," Lucas said. "I think they've got her in there." He stopped and leaned over, taking a moment to regain his energy. When a vehicle came tearing around the corner, it was the detective. Lucas hopped in the back and pointed in the direction the vehicle had gone.

"Go, go, go!" With Top Hat with him, the vehicle sped down the road.

It took four blocks before they saw the vehicle. "That's it," Lucas said.

As if sensing it had been spotted, it took a hard left at the next corner. They followed, and it took a hard right. Lucas swore. He pulled out his phone and called Tanya. "She isn't answering, but I think maybe we can track her via her cell phone."

The cop beside him said, "Give me the number."

Lucas reeled it off.

"We'll start a trace on it right now."

"Okay," Lucas said.

The guy turned to look at him and said, "Looks like we need to drop you off at the hospital."

"Not until we find her," he said. "But if anybody's got something I can use to staunch the blood flow, that would be helpful."

The cop in the passenger seat handed him a thick stack of disposable napkins. He packed them against his wound. "That helps," he said. "Thanks."

"Need to get that bleeding stopped. Otherwise, I *am* dropping you off at the hospital," the detective said.

"It's slowing down," Lucas said. He swore gently under his breath because the bleeding was slowing down, but the pain wasn't. It was still as nasty and as sharp and as biting as ever.

They took several more corners looking for the vehicle, but it was gone. Up ahead was a small parking lot. The detective pulled in, and Lucas listened as they organized a roadblock over a ten-block radius around them. But he just knew they were too late.

CHAPTER 15

TANYA WOKE UP in complete darkness, only to find something over her eyes, a bandage of some kind, and there was enough room for her eyelids to shift ever-so-slightly so she could see shadows below and above.

She couldn't move her hands or her feet. They were tied up too. She groaned softly, afraid to let anyone know she was conscious. She tried to shift, but it wasn't possible as her body was jammed into a tight space. She wiggled a bit, trying to ease the pain in her shoulders, but all it did was make it worse.

She rolled back into the position she'd been in and lay here, trying to establish what had happened. She tested her hands, trying to release them, but they were tied tight. And so were her feet. She swore softly. Although she was small, she had never tried to pull off that trick where people swung their hands tied behind them up and under their butt, then slid their legs through, all without getting stuck halfway.

She had no doubt Lucas was searching for her, and she would be rescued. She would not give up hope. Not now.

He had to know, to realize, that they'd found each other again. She might have been the one who had taken a sideways path, but it wasn't one she was willing to stay on anymore. She wanted him in her life, and that was just the way it was. These assholes wouldn't be allowed to stop her either. Not after everything she'd been through.

She struggled to breathe, the air stale and harsh. She figured she had to be in the back seat of a vehicle, but she didn't know where. If she could see, maybe she could figure out how to get out of here. But again, with her hands behind her back, it was almost impossible. She twisted as she tried to shift her hands below her bum. That took maneuvering, but, by stretching herself completely flat and then bringing her knees right up to her chest, she managed it.

She groaned, feeling her shoulders tug with the movements. She gasped with the effort as she slid her hands up the backside of her legs, wondering how she was supposed to get her ankles through. She brought her knees up high, past her head and dropped her feet down. With her hands in front now, she pulled the bandage off her eyes. Immediately, she felt better.

There was nothing quite like the victim mentality when you were completely susceptible to having your senses dulled when lying in darkness, tied up, waiting for somebody to come and talk to you or do whatever it was they had plans for.

With the bandage off, she saw she was, indeed, in the back of a vehicle. It was an SUV with a hatch. She sat up slowly and peered over the back seat and saw she was in a garage. On top of that she was alone.

She rolled her way over the back seat and opened the door and half fell out onto the garage floor. She closed the door softly. She didn't know how to get out of the garage without raising her kidnappers' awareness. She still had her phone, and that was one hell of a thing.

She sent a text to Lucas. **Got out of SUV. Don't know where I am.**

The response came back immediately with a buzz too loud, and she shut off the ringer. Crouched behind the SUV, she didn't know what to do. But she didn't dare open the big garage door. She crept around to the side door and opened it a hair's breadth. Sunlight streamed in. But there were no shouts at her. She opened it a little farther and slipped out, closing it silently behind her.

She looked around for a place to hide, and, seeing trees ahead, she hobbled toward them. She wouldn't go anywhere fast, and that was a huge problem.

She turned to look back at the garage, wondering if she'd seen anything that would loosen her bonds. She hopped back, opened the door and hopped in again, feeling like she was making so much noise that everybody a block away must hear her. There was a workbench up at the front of the garage, with gas tanks and oil and various things there. She grabbed a hand saw and sawed through the ties at her ankles and then awkwardly worked to get her wrists apart. With the bonds off, she picked up the pieces of the cable ties so her kidnappers wouldn't know and slipped back out the side door and bolted for the trees.

As soon as she cleared the trees, she kept going. The last thing she wanted was for anybody coming behind her to realize she had escaped. She'd always been a good runner, although she was out of practice, but it didn't take long to put several blocks between her and her kidnappers. She glanced back at the street sign and saw she was at the corner of Hemlock and Birch.

She texted that to Lucas and kept running. She never heard anybody behind her. There was a park up ahead. She slipped behind a bush and sat down where she could keep an eye on anybody coming. As soon as she could speak, she called Lucas and said, "I made it to a park just a few blocks away from that house."

"We're on the way," he said.

She almost cried with joy. "Hurry, hurry," she said. "I'm so scared they'll find me."

"We're almost there," he said, only to add in a sharp voice, "Did he hurt you?"

"Knocked me out," she said. "Enough that I didn't know where I'd gone—" Hearing an odd sound beside her, she stopped talking and crouched down low. She spotted two men walking toward her.

She whispered into the phone. "Two men walking my way."

"You stay tight," he said. "Hunker down low. Don't make a sound. We're almost there."

She gave a silent but broken laugh. "I don't know if these are the same men or not, but they're walking into the park in business suits."

"Business suits don't sound right," he said.

"It was a pretty fancy house," she said. "I don't know what's going on. But I don't want anybody else getting their hands on me."

"Did you leave a blood trail?" he asked urgently.

She swore and said, "I don't know. I didn't even think of it."

"Check. Are you bleeding?"

"My shoulder," she said. "Maybe my face. It's pretty swollen. Blood's coming off my fingers, but I don't think there's enough blood for a trail."

"Unless they've got a dog with them. Do they?"

"I can't see through the bush, and I don't want to move."

"We're coming," he said.

She went silent, ended the call and sent him a text. **I'm still here. They're close, too close for comfort.**

She hunkered down as low as she could go and waited. It was all too reminiscent of the last time she had done this. And she'd been caught, beaten, and woke up in the back of a vehicle parked in some strange house. This time she'd do a lot to avoid that again. From where she hid, she could see one of the men, standing with his hands on his hips as he surveyed the area.

"I doubt she went this far," the second man said.

"Maybe not, but we can't take the chance," the first man said.

Just then a vehicle drove into the parking lot, and she watched as a family got out, kids shrieking, and a family dog bailed from the back, barking incessantly. The two men looked at each other, nodded and moved away. She sagged back in relief and closed her eyes.

She sent Lucas a text. **They moved to end of park. They were looking for me. Watch for two men in suits.**

He texted back. **We see them. Watch out. We're coming.**

From where she was, she could see the men walking, and then a vehicle pulled up beside them, and somebody grabbed one and then the other, and both men were bent over the hood of the vehicle.

She wanted to straighten up, but she didn't know which side had just grabbed the men because it was yet another black SUV. Then Lucas hurried toward her, pressing something thick against his shoulder, and it was soaked in blood. She bolted out of the brush and raced to him. He wrapped his arms around her as she slammed into him, a groan of pain coming from his chest.

"Oh, I'm sorry. I'm sorry," she cried out, her hand going to the bloody bandage. "They hurt you!"

"Yes, but they also hurt you," he said gently and held her close, kissing her forehead. "It's over."

"Is it?" she asked. Just then a dog jumped up on her, and she cried out as she looked down to see Top Hat on his back legs. She laughed and gave him a great big hug, kissing him. "Top Hat was great. He bit the guy who kidnapped me. I think that's why the guy hit me. He was so angry. He kept trying to hit Top Hat, but he kept dancing away. Then Top Hat found me again. So we owe Top Hat a lot."

Lucas squatted in front of the dog and gave Top Hat a good scrub on the face and neck. Top Hat licked his face.

"What will we do with him?" she asked.

"I suggest we keep him," he said with a chuckle. "You might not want a family, but maybe, if we start with a canine family, you'll be a little more amiable to having kids."

She laughed. "I'll never have a problem having a canine family," she said.

"Tanya?" he asked.

Just the way he said her name had her studying him, wondering what serious business he was about to bring up. What could be more serious than the family angle that had broken them up to begin with? But she had to know. She wouldn't give up Lucas so easily this time. She would fight for him, with him, to keep him. "What is it, Lucas?"

"Would you want to take in your brothers?"

She had thought about it, but mostly she had been working through her own problems with her mother.

"I mean, after your mother passes?"

She gave a one-arm shrug. "You saw them in there. They

didn't even respond to me as I walked out, too busy with their computer game."

Lucas shook her gently by her shoulders, bent down to get to her eye level. "Remember what I said earlier? These are fourteen-year-old twin boys, interested in sports, girls and video games. And they are like men everywhere, with a single-minded laser focus on one thing at a time." He laughed as Tanya frowned. "You women multitask. We men deal with one thing at a time. Like me with my hospital stay."

"Okay?" But her confusion was evident in that one word.

"Your brothers were focused on their computer game. Don't take it as anything more than that."

"But taking on even one teenage boy is such a daunting task." She faced Lucas fully now. "I raised mostly girls. Boys are different. Just like you said."

"Yeah, but you'd have help this time."

She almost danced a jig, but she needed clarity first. "You want to help me raise Tom and Tennessee? Really?"

Lucas pointed at Top Hat. "I'm a sucker for lost causes."

She hesitated; it was all happening so fast. So many emotions tumbled through her.

"You don't have to decide now. You have months for that. Then, when the time comes, you can have a face-to-face discussion with your brothers. You can all discuss it and decide. And I bet you'll have their full attention then. Okay?"

She smiled, and it hurt, her hand coming automatically to her face. "Do you think we can go home now?"

He straightened again, reached out a hand and grabbed hers. "We have to go to the hospital. I need to get my shoulder looked at, and you need to get your eye looked at."

She stared at him in surprise. "I can see just fine."

"Maybe," he said. "But your face is really puffy."

And that was what they did.

By the time she was treated and released from the hospital, they were back to looking for each other again. The cops had been there multiple times, talked to her and talked to him, and the hospital had separated them, as they each needed different treatments. When Lucas finally walked out of the emergency area, she was at the front desk, filling out forms.

"Are you ready to go?" he asked, his voice slurred and his energy fading. He would collapse soon. "I need to go to bed. I've been given a shot that's likely to knock me flat on my ass for the next twelve hours."

She looked at him. "We don't have wheels, but I think one of the police officers can give us a ride home."

"Good," he said. "Where is Top Hat?"

"One of the cops was nice enough to watch over him, to let him get a bathroom break and to get him some water. He said he'd wait for us outside."

They walked out of the hospital to see one of the cop cars pulling up in front. Detective Madison hopped out and introduced himself. He shook their hands and said, "You two look like you've seen better days."

"Right?" she said. "Please tell me that you got everyone?"

He nodded. "The two businessman who came after you? They were the ones at the top of the dogfighting rings. They don't generally get their hands dirty, but you disappeared from their house."

"And that SUV?"

"We're running forensics on it right now, but I'm pretty

sure it's the one that ran down your friend Alice."

Tanya cried out, her hand going to her mouth as she stared at him.

"Yes, they are also associated with your former boss too. He's been picked up for questioning, along with the rest of the staff. We will have a talk with them tomorrow."

She nodded ever-so-slowly. "And Claire?"

His face was grim as he tilted his head and firmed his mouth. "As far as we can tell, yes, as a dispatcher, she overheard something about the dogfighting ring, … but we have some pieces to put together still."

She nodded. "Any chance somebody can give us a ride to my place? Lucas will drop here very quickly."

The detective nodded. "Come on. I'll take you."

Top Hat, who'd been lying close by, raced over. She watched as Lucas bent down to give the dog lots of love. "Do you mind if he comes with us? He saved my life. He's coming to my place."

"Sure. Why not?" the detective said. "Bullet wounds aren't to be trifled with."

The three of them piled into the back seat, and she watched worriedly as Lucas's head rolled to the side. "You hang on, Lucas. We're almost home."

"Maybe he should have stayed in the hospital," the detective said.

"No," Lucas said faintly. "Me and hospitals don't do well."

"It doesn't matter," the detective said. "Sometimes you need to be there."

"All I need now is sleep."

"Well, that's what we'll do," Tanya said. "Let's get you home."

When they got to her place, she opened the car door, looked at the detective and said, "I might need a hand getting him up to my apartment."

He nodded and helped Lucas out of the vehicle, where he stood wavering on his feet, but he looked determinedly at the door and took several strong strides. The detective looped an arm around his ribs, threw his arm over his shoulder and said, "Come on. Let's go."

She led Top Hat to her place, and they slowly climbed the stairs, not for the first time. She was wishing again they had an elevator here. Finally upstairs, she unlocked the door and motioned for the detective to help Lucas in. "Take him straight through to the bedroom, if you wouldn't mind."

With Top Hat inside, and the door closed, she turned around to see the detective leaving her bedroom. "Is he out?"

He nodded. "He'll be out for a while."

She smiled at him. "And that's fine. We're home, and we're safe, and hopefully this is all over with."

"It's over on your end," he said. "Definitely we have lots of questions, and we'll have to get several statements from you as we tie things up."

"You got everybody involved in the dogfighting?"

"Seems so," he said. "If not, we've still got a wider net we're running. It's a big operation, and we've taken down over thirty-five participants. We've also got the hit-and-run driver. I don't know if there will be any charges for what happened to you at your job. If possible, we'll add it to all the others, but you know it's only the big charges that'll stick."

"Get everybody on the murder charge," she said. "Unfortunately abuse of animals and criminal betting rings like that won't have anywhere near as much emphasis as the murder, so nail as many as you can for that. My job loss isn't an issue. I've gotten more out of this than I ever expected."

"We'll see." He smiled, shook her hand and said, "I'll contact you tomorrow. Right now you need sleep too."

She checked her watch and realized it was almost ten p.m. She groaned. "I am so ready to go to bed."

She thanked him, then locked the door behind him and gave Top Hat some water. She didn't know what to do about dog food but found some ham and cheese, so she chopped that up and gave it to him. He ate that in two gulps, then still stared at her. So she made him some peanut butter on bread, and he devoured that. "I'm sorry, buddy. Tomorrow we'll find you some more food."

He didn't seem to be too bothered once the food was gone, and he headed into the bedroom, looking for Lucas. She was in the same state. She pulled the blanket off the end of the bed and laid it on the floor for Top Hat, who stretched out.

It was all she could do to brush her teeth and to strip down before she fell over. She wanted to remove some of Lucas's clothing, but he was a dead weight. She managed to get his shoes and jeans off, but that was it. She rolled over with another blanket and crashed.

She woke up several times in the night as Lucas rolled, shifted and moaned.

She shook him gently and whispered, "Take more pain-killers." She gave him two of the pills he'd been given from the hospital. He popped them in his mouth and drank some water. With her help, they stripped off the bloody T-shirt he still wore. She pulled the blankets back up and covered him. She snuggled against him, and they slept again.

LUCAS WOKE UP, feeling not so bad this time, and rolled over to see Tanya curled up beside him. He smiled and tucked her in close.

"You shouldn't be awake," she said.

"I'm feeling pretty good," he said.

"In that case, Top Hat probably has to go outside."

He swore. But, as he shifted to look down at Top Hat, the dog sat, staring at him over the end of the bed, hope in his eyes. "Yeah, that's exactly what he needs," he said. "I'll be back." He slipped out of bed and pulled on his jeans and took Top Hat outside.

He walked him to the area at the back of the apartment building and let him do his business. After that, he led him slowly back inside and up the stairs. He searched the apartment for food and found little. He made some toast and eggs and fed it to Top Hat. He also gave him some ham and cheese. Top Hat seemed to inhale whatever was presented to him. "It's dog food after this, buddy," he said.

Top Hat gave a bark. Lucas put on coffee, and, when he had a second load of scrambled eggs and toast ready, he piled it on a large platter and awkwardly brought it into the bedroom. His shoulder was holding, especially if he didn't use that arm. Tanya was just waking up again.

She shifted on the bed, sitting up, tucking the sheet around her chest. Yawning, she said, "Coffee and breakfast in bed? Who'd have thought?"

"Yesterday I wouldn't have," he said. "But I'm pleased to be in this position right now. I'm sore. I'm stiff, and I'm feeling not as good as I would like to, but, hey, we're alive. We have Top Hat with us, and we slept in a real bed so ..."

She chuckled and shifted again as he placed the platter of food down on the center of the bed. Top Hat jumped up and lay down at the end.

Lucas groaned. "We'll have to work on your manners, buddy."

But he didn't beg, he just lay here and watched as they had their breakfast.

"We have to get dog food," she said. "The only thing I gave him last night was ham and cheese—oh, and some bread and peanut butter."

"Well, he got eggs, toast, ham and cheese this morning," Lucas said, chuckling. Just then he had the crust of his buttery toast in his hand, and it was the last piece. He reached across, and Top Hat inhaled it. "This is a really bad habit, isn't it?"

"Really bad habit," Tanya said, laughing. "It's hard to blame us when we don't have anything else to feed him though."

As soon as the food was gone, Lucas got up, gave the sheet a bit of a shake and lay down. He pulled her into his arms. "I'm so glad you survived," he said. "I'll have nightmares for decades from that."

"So will I," she announced. She studied the bandage on his shoulder. "I'm so sorry you got hurt."

"Ditto," he said. He leaned down and kissed her gently on the temple. "What will we do now?"

"You mean *now, right now?*" she asked in a teasing voice. "Because I've never, ever heard that you were slow to figure out what to do with an almost naked woman in a bed. Or were you talking about our *future now?*"

"Well, I was talking about our future," he said chuckling. "But, hey, if we'll talk about *right now*, I'm up for that too."

She slid a hand across his muscular chest and down his abs to his boxers, her hand gliding along the cloth. "You are definitely up for that," she said, laughing. "Never knew you when you weren't."

"That's because there's absolutely nothing about you that I don't adore," he said. "Even when we were apart these last many months, I always hoped we would get back together. I never went out with anybody else because you held my heart."

She continued stroking him through his boxers, increasing the pressure to make him squirm. "I wasn't anywhere near as astute. I figured it was over, and I'd lost the best thing in my life. I knew I still loved you, and, on my better days, I hoped deep down we still had a chance but ..."

"You haven't lost me," he whispered. "I'm not going anywhere." He shifted gently so his shoulder didn't feel the same pain and pressure and rolled on top of her. "Unless, of course, you want more time to yourself to think," he asked, pulling up on his good elbow.

She shook her head. "No, I've been a fool, and I came close to losing the only thing that really mattered."

He bent his head to kiss her gently. "I'm glad to hear that," he said. "I have to go home a couple times over the next few months, but I really don't have anything keeping me there."

"Oh, look at that? You're hardly a good prospect then, are you?" she teased. "No job, no home ..."

"Then there's you, with no decent job and an apartment that doesn't even have an elevator," he joked.

She smiled, sliding her arms around his neck and whispered, "So maybe we'll find a new place together and start to work out these problems."

"That's a plan," he whispered, and he took her lips in a long, slow kiss.

She moaned softly beneath him.

He shifted again, sliding down lower, his one arm holding up his weight, the other one moving gently but not with too much freedom.

She shook her head when he finally lifted his head and whispered, "Roll over."

He stretched out on his back. "What do you have in mind?"

"I have in mind a method that won't hurt your shoulder," she said. She gently stripped his boxers down his hips, then kicked off her panties. She straddled his hips.

Starting at her wrists, he grazed his fingers up her arms and gently cupped her breasts, squeezing and teasing her flesh. "You were always so perfect," he said. "I had no idea just how perfect the female form was until I met you."

She smiled. "You lie beautifully," she said. "But thank you."

He chuckled.

She kissed him again and then again.

He wanted to wrap his arms around her and pull her close, but she pulled away, letting her fingers and lips trail over his shoulder, pressing her lips gently around the bandage. She swirled her tongue around each nipple as she slid her hand down his abs to play with his belly button. "We were always so good together," she said.

"*Mmm*," he said, his fingers drifting through her hair, pulling on her long strands. "We still are good together. Don't you forget that."

"And will we always be?" she asked, straightening up and

looking at him, knowing the shadows of fear were still in her eyes.

He smiled and whispered, "Absolutely." He tugged her down closer where he could kiss her. "Even when we were apart, we knew we should be together."

She stretched out across his body and let her own mind shut down while her body and heart took over. Before long, she rose up to sit astride his hard body, loving the feel, loving the motion, loving the movement, just being with him and having this all back again when she'd come so close to losing everything. She slowly took him in and whispered, "Dear God, I didn't want to lose this—you again."

"You were never in danger of losing me," he said, his hands holding her hips firm as she gently rode him. "This was what we were always meant to have. This is who we were always meant to be."

She smiled, bent over, using his chest to brace her hands and picked up the pace. When she couldn't stand it anymore, she cried out as her body rocked with explosions.

His hands held her hips firm as he surged up twice and exploded inside her.

She rolled over so she was right beside him on the bed. "Perfect," she whispered. "As always."

He cuddled her close and smiled. "Just think. We have a beautiful future ahead of us."

She hugged him closer and murmured, "Absolutely. It's been a long and difficult road, but we're here finally."

EPILOGUE

"**A**NOTHER ONE BITES the dust, huh?" Geir sat with his feet up on the boardroom table and smiled at the rest of the team. "I can't believe these K9 guys are all getting hitched, and most of them are keeping the dogs," he said.

"And one murder and an attempted murder have been solved at the same time," Badger said, shaking his head. "That's a doubly awesome job."

"Who'd have thought that the one girlfriend, who worked in dispatch, had overheard the dirty cops discussing the dogfights and their involvement. After that, they couldn't take the chance she'd talk so took her out, then her roommate. They planned to knock off Tanya as well but were just waiting for a better time. In the meantime one of the accountants who worked with Tanya had heard about Tanya's girlfriend's involvement in the dogfighting and didn't want to keep Tanya close, in case she found out anything else—like how the firm was laundering money for the dogfighting rings—so got rid of her too. Doesn't that just make you love people?"

"Not much," Badger said. "It's not what we expected on a mission to save one War Dog. Yet Lucas is responsible for saving more than 160 dogs. And we especially didn't plan the matchmaking success on this op."

Kat came in, a cup of coffee in her hand, and sat down

beside them. "Might not be what we had planned or what you guys had planned," she said, "but it's all good news."

"Says the woman who arranged all our weddings," Geir said, chuckling.

Badger watched the color wash over her cheeks but grabbed her fingers in his and whispered, "Thank God."

She beamed at him. "You guys can hate me until doomsday," she said, "or pretend to, but you know that you're all much better off the way you are now. *Happily married.*"

"Oh, we're not arguing with that," Erick said. "I think we're all happy little pigs in our blankets, but we have more dogs to look after." He spread the files around. "Take a look and see if there's anybody here that we know of to match up with another dog. The commander called to check in the other day. Now we have another success story to tell him. But I'm sure he's wondering what's taking us so long."

"There's no time frame involved," Geir said. He opened the file in front of him and flipped through the pages. "Hell, this one's over in Iraq still."

Badger lifted his head. "Seriously?"

He nodded, his face glum. "The poor dog's probably dead and gone by now."

"Well, that's an interesting state of affairs," Erick said.

Badger looked at him. "Why is that?"

"Because Parker is heading there on a compassionate leave trip. His brother was killed in action. He's planning on escorting his body home. But that doesn't mean, while he's there, he doesn't have a day or two to track down the dog."

"The dog was lost at the military base?" Badger asked.

Geir flipped through the pages. "Yes. And, once it's off the base, it's no longer their problem. To give them their due credit, everybody did search for the dog. They wondered if it had been stolen. It was decommissioned and due to fly home the next day. Apparently the dog arrived at the airport but disappeared while waiting to be picked up. Its whereabouts after its arrival at the hangar is a mystery. There are discrepancies in the witness statements. They are thinking that maybe somebody close to the airport may have kidnapped the dog."

"Does Commander Cross really want us to go over there and look into this one?" Geir asked, shaking his head. "That's a bit out of the boundaries, isn't it?"

"If it wasn't for Parker heading over there tomorrow, I wouldn't think of looking into this one," Erick said. "If Parker can find the dog, he can bring him home with him as well."

Badger nodded. "Where's Parker now?"

"He's packing, I think. His brother, Jerry, and his crew were taken out by an IED. Jerry's best friend was part of his unit, and Sandy, his best friend's sister, is heading over there with him."

Grins popped up around the table.

Erick nodded. "I know what you're thinking," he said. "She's military too. I think she's a nurse in California. She also asked for special permission to go over there."

"Of course. Bringing family home is important to everyone."

"Do you want to call him?" Badger asked Erick. "You seem to know him the best."

"He's been around for a while, but, yeah, I used to know him in the military too," Erick said. "Unlike the rest of us, he's not missing a body part."

"Unless he's missing his heart," Jager said. "As in pining

for his brother. Maybe it's a good thing this Sandy is going over there too. It's a tough trip for anyone, and it would help to not be alone."

"It's a shit trip no matter who goes with you," Erick said, but he already had his phone out and was dialing.

Geir watched in surprise. "Is he on your contact list?"

Erick nodded. "Yeah, he is."

There was silence for a moment, then Erick was giving his condolences first before adding, "I heard you're heading over to Iraq tomorrow. What base?"

Erick nodded, while they all watched. Then he grinned. He motioned with his hand for the file in front of Geir. "Look. We have an odd request. Commander Cross dropped a dozen files on us filled with K9 agents who served their time and, for one reason or another, have been retired and then lost. We have one that disappeared between the base and the airport in Iraq. We're trying to get him home and settled into a decent life here." Erick was silent as he listened for a short while. Then he said, "Oh, you heard about him?"

He looked around the room. "Great. Do you have any K9 experience?"

Erick frowned and nodded. The others waited. "Okay. If you've got an extra day, and you don't mind taking a look, we would really appreciate being able to tell the commander we have found the dog and have brought him home and have set him up some place worthy of a War Dog. If that's something you feel you can do, that would be awesome. But we do understand if you can't. Obviously anything to do with your brother comes first. Again our condolences on your loss."

The conversation continued for a few minutes, and Geir and Badger exchanged looks. And then Erick ended the call.

He looked around the table. "Well, he's game. He said he has a couple days over there, and he would look up some friends by the base. And, believe it or not," he added with a note of satisfaction, "he's going to FOB Wild, where the dog went missing."

"*FOB Wild?* That's one of the forward operating bases in the northern Iraqi province of Nineveh, a few miles outside of Tal Afar," Badger said in surprise as he reached for the folder to double-check the location where the dog had gone missing for himself. "That's perfect. Maybe somebody there knows something."

"I hope so," Erick said. "Parker's just leaving the military himself. I think he's done in a couple weeks. Been on medical leave and not going back."

"Understood," Badger said. "Not easy for anybody when losing someone so close to you."

"True enough," Geir said. "Let's just see what happens. Maybe we'll get lucky again."

"You mean, maybe he'll get lucky," Jager said with a grin.

All the men laughed, and Erick nodded. "Luck comes in many forms," he said. "Let's hope he finds one form that suits him."

PARKER CUTTER HOPPED into his borrowed rig, checked the GPS for directions and backed out of the parking lot. He realized he already knew the direction, as he'd been here before, and slowly drove onto the main road. He'd had lunch with a few friends as soon as he'd arrived. They'd picked him up and taken him into town with them, but, now hours later, he'd left them there with other friends and had taken one of the rigs to head to the base. He needed a few moments to get his head together. With any luck this stretch of the journey would give it to him. This was a crappy trip. The only good thing was he had a couple friends he was looking forward to seeing on base too.

He had ten more days in the service, and five of those were for compassionate leave. He'd wondered about taking all his days here, but, as the compassionate leave was due to his brother's death, it hardly seemed like a good time to tack on holidays. He was only in Iraq for a short time—just long enough to bring his brother home to the US—then long enough to help his father bury Jerry back home.

Military life for Parker was almost done, and it seemed like a lifetime to get to that point. He'd never even considered it for years, but this year, … with his accident, … followed by his brother's death, … Parker had hit a wall. He wasn't even sure what the hell he would do now. He just knew he was starting a new life—albeit one without his brother.

He'd had a bad accident when the vehicle he was in had rolled, got his leg pinned and was now assigned to a desk job he couldn't stand.

There was a chance of more surgery to help build up his shoulder as well. Something to do with muscles and the scapula. He wasn't prepared to do that now, or maybe ever, but he could get it done whether on active leave or not.

What he didn't like was the desk job. If he could get out and be mobile, it wouldn't be so bad, but being at a desk made him feel like he was retired from life.

Maybe if he hadn't come from a high-level active military team, he wouldn't feel like he was secondhand goods.

Now his life was just a reminder of the one left behind because he couldn't do the job anymore.

As he drove along the road, his brain was consumed with the issues about his future. He thought about Sandy and her brother. Parker had lost Jerry, and Sandy has lost Jeremy. Both of their brothers had died at the same time on the same mission. So Parker and Sandy were both here for a couple days before they took off.

There would be short ceremonies for the men killed in action, in service to their country, and then they were all heading back home. And it sucked. It sucked big time. Which was why, when Erick suggested Parker look for the poor dog, Samson, Parker agreed. Samson was supposed to go home and retire but had somehow gone missing at the military airport. It was that *somehow gone missing* part that really bothered Parker.

Because that *somehow gone missing* phrase sounded like a military error or one of those stupid accounting mistakes that had the dog sent someplace other than where he was intended to be. It also bothered Parker because there was a chance somebody had taken the dog deliberately. Well-trained animals were worth a lot of money. War Dogs were bred for skill, endurance, intelligence and size. They were a huge asset and were coveted by others.

Last thing he wanted was to be in the open on enemy lines to face his own War Dogs attacking him. He couldn't imagine how confusing that would be for the animals too.

He had another twenty-five minutes to FOB Wild. He was going at a fast clip, but he wasn't late—he was not on a time frame at all. He should meander, enjoy this last visit. But he was here for the worst reason possible. He wanted to race through it, so it was done and over with, and he could begin to heal. Time was the only way to get through this horrible loss, and he was afraid he'd forever associate this part of the world with Jerry.

His truck started wobbling, and the next second he felt a hard bang, and the tire was gone. Swearing softly, he pulled off to the side of the road and hopped out. Sure enough, his back left tire was gone, down the road a piece. He needed to change the tire, and, well, that was never anybody's favorite job.

He had the vehicle jacked up, lifted from the ground, the old tire off and the new one on, and was tightening the lugs when he heard another vehicle approaching.

He looked up to see Sandy, Jeremy's sister, who'd flown in with Parker on the same plane but had soon left with two women. She got out of the jeep and ran over to him. "We left ahead of you," she said. "But we ended up going into town for lunch and lost track of time."

He smiled and said, "Good. I went into town too. Should have stayed longer. I would much rather have been still socializing than changing a tire." But he was joking, and she knew it.

She smiled. "Well, at least you got it fixed. Do you think it's okay? Is there anything we can do to help?"

"I'm fine," he said, his pride bristling to the surface. He stood, brushed off his pant legs, reached down and picked up the jack and walked to the end of his truck, placing it under the bed. In its spot. He walked back to where the damaged tire had landed and rolled it to the back where he hoisted it into the bed.

The two women with Sandy were dressed in military fatigues. He nodded to them and smiled as he rubbed his hands on a rag, cleaning off the dirt, dust and grime. Sandy explained who he was, and their expressions changed. They reached out, shook his hand and said, "Sorry for your loss."

Even now it choked him up. He muttered, "Thank you." Then motioned at the truck. "Hopefully now it'll get me to the base."

"You go first," the driver of the other vehicle said. "We'll follow to make sure you get there."

Touched, he nodded. "Thanks. I'm not too proud to accept the offer. I doubt there'll be a problem. It's a new tire."

"Yeah, and we all know that doesn't necessarily mean it's a good tire," she said with a touch of humor.

He laughed, tossing the rag in the back of the truck. He walked over to the driver side, slid in and turned the engine on and, with a wave, headed toward the base.

He was surprised Sandy was with them, but then she had probably met a lot of her brother's friends, and she was also military, though she was a nurse stateside. He wasn't even sure where he got that tidbit of information from. Then their brothers had been best friends. This was just as painful a trip for her as it was for him, and, if she had friends to make the trip a little easier, all the better for her.

The time flew as he drove. Once he arrived at the base, he honked his horn and stuck his arm out of his truck to wave his thanks and turned off into the base. He spotted his buddies' vehicles and parked beside them. He knew which barracks they were in, and he'd been assigned one himself. He grabbed his duffel bag, slung it over his shoulder and headed for his friends.

As he stepped inside, he found the entire barracks were empty. Frowning, he picked out his bed, dropped his duffle, left the barracks and headed to the mess tent. He could always count on a cup of coffee, if nothing else.

It was also empty. He checked with the guy behind the counter. "Everybody clear out all of a sudden?" he asked. "I hope it wasn't my arrival."

The guy behind the counter grinned at him. "We're on high alert this morning. Everybody's taken off to check out insurgents, who may or may not have attacked a small group of villagers," he explained.

Parker nodded. "Been there, done that," he said, not surprised. "I presume they went out in waves?"

"They're all over the place," he said. "You know that, as soon as you decide to wait until later to eat, you'll turn around and have two hundred men in here, loading up, and you won't be able to get back to the food for hours."

"I was just coming for coffee. How many hours until food?" Parker asked, checking his watch, trying to mentally calculate the time difference.

"Two hours," the guy replied.

Parker nodded, grabbed a large cup of coffee and a muffin, and walked back to his barracks. He could have sat at a table, but it felt odd. He felt odd. He was still one of them, and yet, in a way not one of them. He'd already handed in his notice. He was here to take his brother home, and then he was almost done.

Ten days. Five of them were for his brother, and yet, how could he explain that to anybody?

He sent a text to Badger. **Here. Arrived. No sign of dog.**

Thanks for the update. And that was it.

What was he supposed to say? They all knew he was here for a tough reason and might start working for Badger, potentially, when he was done. At least Parker had told

Badger that he was available to help if Badger needed anything—yet Parker hadn't decided on a specific direction for himself right now. According to Badger there was always room for another guy at the place, but the Titanium Corp was in New Mexico. Parker was based out of California. Who knew where the hell he'd end up?

He finished his coffee and muffin, tossed away his trash. One thing you were taught to do when you were in the military was to keep your area clean. He headed over to shipping and receiving. As he stepped inside, he smiled at the supply clerk. "I'm here to check on the whereabouts of the dog that went missing."

Her face stiffened. "I can't tell you very much," she said cautiously. "I was told the investigation was closed."

"But the dog hasn't been found, correct?"

"It was seen in town, but I don't know what happened beyond that," she replied curtly. "If it is found, it'll be shipped back stateside. I have standing orders to do that, but until I have the dog ..."

"So, did it go missing here, or did it go missing at the air base?"

"At the air base," she replied, looking at him strangely. "It was a really nice dog too."

"Are you thinking maybe somebody took it?"

"It wouldn't be the first time things go missing," she muttered.

Considering where she worked, he nodded. "Who was the one taking the dog to the base?"

She clicked over to the computer file, brought it up, printed off a page and was about to hand it to him. "I need ID first though."

He looked at her in surprise and pulled out his ID card.

She nodded. "Okay. You're the only one cleared for this information."

He raised an eyebrow.

"Commander Cross called about it," she said with a half smile. "The K9 War Dogs division has been shut down, but you're still checking into a few of his cases, correct?"

He nodded. "At least I can do something worthwhile the last few days before I'm done."

"Are you leaving?" she asked in surprise, her tone almost envious.

"Yes," he said. "I have ten days left. I actually came here to escort my brother's body home, but, while here, I'm looking into Samson's disappearance." He turned with a half wave, grabbed the paper and walked out.

"There you are."

Parker heard and looked up to see his friend Cam.

They shook hands and slapped each other on the back in a half hug.

Parker grinned and said, "I checked the barracks for you, but you weren't there."

"Nah. I was over with the vehicles," he said.

"What do you know about Gorman?" Parker asked.

"What do you want with Gorman?"

"I'm looking into the dog that disappeared."

"That was bizarre," Cam said. "Not that I heard very much about it, just that a dog went missing. Why you?"

"I was asked to," he said with a smile. That was one of the things about the military—there were a lot of secrets, and nobody really expected you to tell them the truth about anything because, more often than not, you couldn't.

"Gorman Manga was on that run with one of his friends, but I can't remember his name. Gorman, actually both of them, are away from the base though. I think they are on leave in Germany," Cam said, frowning.

"His name's really Gorman Manga?"

"Yes," he said with a laugh. "He didn't appreciate it much either."

"Do you know him well enough to ask him about the dog?"

"Sure." Cam pulled out his phone and asked, "What do you want to know?"

"How the dog went missing. Apparently it was crated. Did the entire crate get picked up and moved? Is he sure it was latched? Did he sell it or …"

Cam's eyebrows shot up. "Okay." He walked over a few steps to make the call. Parker moved in closer so he could hear the conversation. Cam ended the call and turned to Parker. "We caught him still awake. The dog was crated. The team turned away, loading up everything else. The dog would go up front with them. When they finished loading all the gear and went back to the trolley where the dog was, the front gate was open, and the crate was empty."

"And he never saw anybody hanging around the place?"

Cam shook his head. "He says not. It was him and two other guys loading, and the ground crew."

"I wonder why this dog."

"Or any dog for that matter," Cam said. "He may have gone in another shipment. Or the door may have come open, and he escaped on his own."

"Maybe. I guess those are possibilities. As long as the paperwork was still in order."

"If any of the ground crew were responsible for the lapse, and they catch the dog, I'm sure they would ship him back over again and worry about the paperwork later."

"Pretty sloppy though," Parker said. "If they get caught, they get shit for the way they handled it."

"It's just a delayed shipment. Hardly a big deal for anybody except the dog."

"In this case, the dog was going to an adopted family," Parker said. "I wonder if that has something to do with it."

"I don't know," Cam said. "Anything is possible. When are you leaving again?"

"Day after tomorrow," Parker replied. "After the short ceremony for Jeremy and Jerry tomorrow, then we fly back with them in the evening."

Cam's face dropped. "That was a shit deal," he said. "I'm so sorry."

"Me too," Parker said. "If it isn't my brother, it'd be somebody's else kin for sure."

Cam nodded. "But you're almost done. I can't believe that. No second thoughts?"

Parker shook his head. "No second thoughts. Jerry's and Jeremy's deaths were the last straw. I'm tired of all the dying."

"Gotcha. You still need plans for the future," Cam said.

"No. I don't," Parker said. "I really don't."

They talked a little more while they walked. Parker looked at one of the names on the manifest in front of him for the dog and said, "What about this other guy, Manfred? Tobey Manfred."

"Tobey's a good guy. He's over in Germany with Gorman."

"Okay. And it's only the dog that was lost. Correct?"

"I can ask Gorman if anything else went missing, but I think it was just the dog." He sent a text this time. As they walked, Cam said, "It's almost time for food. We have to get there early. Otherwise, you know what happens."

"Sure. Let's go eat. I had coffee and a muffin, but that's been an hour already."

"By the time we get back there and get into line and get through the line, it'll be grub-eating time," Cam said.

They turned around and headed back through the camp base to the cafeteria. Parker greeted several men he knew as he walked up the line, but only Cam he knew well enough to visit with.

When they were done eating, he looked up, surprised to see Sandy in the middle of the room, searching for a place to sit. He motioned to her. She smiled and walked over. "Hey. Fancy meeting you here. Mind if I join you?"

"No. Not at all," he said. He introduced her to Cam and explained why she was there.

Cam offered his condolences. "I'm sorry for your loss."

She nodded. "It's tough. You don't want to tell anybody why you are here because, after a while, they just don't know what to say."

Cam stood, smiled at them and said, "I'll check in with you later, Parker. I've got meetings to go to." And he strode off.

Sandy smiled at Parker. "I'm sorry. I didn't mean to chase him away."

"You didn't," he said. "It feels odd to be here, doesn't it? Like we're a guest but not quite."

"I was just thinking that as well," she said. "I did a couple tours over here, and now that I'm back for this short time, it feels like I don't really belong. I don't have places to go or people to see."

"Neither do I," he said with perfect understanding. "I wish we could go back tonight."

She leaned forward. "Me too," she said. "When they said we'd fly in tonight on the military plane and then we'd leave several days later, I was like, why can't we do this trip faster? This isn't a trip I want to prolong. I'm good to have it all done in one day. This is tough enough. We still have the funerals to go through at home."

"I know," he said. "That'll be a whole other level of hell. On top of that, ... I'm leaving the military. I only have ten days left."

She slowly put her fork down. "Don't tell me your brother was the last straw?"

He nodded. "A big part of it but there were other reasons too. Why?" And then he knew. "You too?"

"Yes. I've been thinking about it for a long time though," she confessed. "My brother was the one who kept me in all these years. He was such a strong believer, and I am too. Coronado has been good for me, but I was thinking it was time to go into the private sector."

"Not too many people go into the private sector," he said with half a laugh.

"Which is also why I wasn't so sure I wanted to go back into that, but I know some people that maybe I can work with. A couple private hospitals."

"Right," he said. "I do know somebody connected to a private hospital, but I don't know if they're looking for employees."

"This is my last official job. Then I don't know what ..." she said with a note of bitterness. She put her knife and fork down, pinched the bridge of her nose, whispering, "I'm sorry."

He grasped her other hand in his and said, "Don't. Don't apologize. We both lost somebody who matters to us.

This process is difficult enough. We can't try to hide our feelings. We have to acknowledge them and carry on."

She gave him a half smile. "I don't even want food, but, in the back of my head, I keep hearing a voice that says, *You need your strength. Eat.*"

He agreed. "I can't see any reason to argue with that common sense. I ate a whole plate of food, and I don't even know what it was."

She nodded and took several bites. She looked like she was feeling better. She lifted her head from her focus on the plate and said, "Did you ever learn anything about the dog?"

"I spoke to someone. A couple of someones. While they were loading the luggage, somebody opened the hatch and let the dog out," he said. "Other than that, I don't know."

"Right. So, any cameras? Anybody have any idea who was hanging around at the time?"

"I need to go to the air base and talk to the ground crew," he said. "The men who took the dog to the air base are on leave in Germany. Although, according to this statement, they both said they saw the dog there."

"Any chance they're lying?" she asked in a low tone, looking around to make sure nobody heard them.

He felt a start of surprise. "That's an interesting thought. I hadn't really considered it, but they are both backing up the same story. I guess it depends what the ground crew says."

"Depends on which ground crew. You may have to go there a couple times."

He glanced at his watch and said, "I thought I'd go tonight. The ceremony is at noon, and then we leave." He looked at the food left on her plate. "You did well."

"I feel like puking," she admitted.

"Maybe some fresh air will help. You want to drive with me to the air base again?"

She nodded. "Sure. Why not? It's not like I've got anything here to do. We're both at loose ends, so, if we go together, we might achieve something."

"Maybe one of our last good deeds while we're in the military is to find this dog," he said.

"The dog has already been decommissioned, hasn't it?"

"Yes. If that's what they call it," he said. "He was supposed to go to a foster family in California."

"We're heading back to California, so, if that's the case, maybe we can take him back with us?"

"Maybe," he said. "The trouble is, we might get attached and not want to give him up."

"If you find it and rescue it, I'm sure you'll get priority on keeping it," she said, laughing.

He grinned. "I'm not sure I'm ready for a dog. I don't have a job after ten days from now."

"Join the club," she said, laughing. They got up from the table, and she looped her arm through his. "We're both at very new stages in our lives."

"Right." He nodded. He would add, and decided not to, that, in order to have their new starts, they first had to close the door on their old life. And unfortunately, they would both be closing the door without their brothers.

This concludes Book 5 of The K9 Files: Lucas.

Read about Parker: The K9 Files, Book 6

THE K9 FILES: PARKER (BOOK #6)

Heading back to Iraq was never in Parker's plans ...

But, when his brother is killed in action, he makes the journey to bring his brother back home to his final resting place.

When one of the K9 War Dogs disappears at the military airport in transit, and all attempts to locate him fails, Parker agrees to investigate during the few days he's there.

Sandy is making the same journey as Parker—both of their brothers were killed in the same incident. Both brothers had been the best of friends, but this is the first time she's met Parker. From that initial moment, she realizes something odd is happening in his world. When they find a K9 dog in a rebel stronghold, she's sucked into a much more dangerous trip than one of compassion and grief.

There's a reason why the first investigation didn't turn up anything. ... As Parker rattles cages and shakes up a ring of thieves, the bodies start dropping, one by one.

Book 6 is available now!

To find out more visit Dale Mayer's website.

https://geni.us/DMParkerUniversal

Author's Note

Thank you for reading Lucas: The K9 Files, Book 5! If you enjoyed the book, please take a moment and leave a short review.

Dear reader,

I love to hear from readers, and you can contact me at my website: www.dalemayer.com or at my Facebook author page. To be informed of new releases and special offers, sign up for my newsletter or follow me on BookBub. And if you are interested in joining Dale Mayer's Reader Group, here is the Facebook sign up page.
http://geni.us/DaleMayerFBGroup

Cheers,
Dale Mayer

About the Author

Dale Mayer is a *USA Today* best-selling author, best known for her SEALs military romances, her Psychic Visions series, and her Lovely Lethal Garden cozy series. Her contemporary romances are raw and full of passion and emotion (Broken But ... Mending, Hathaway House series). Her thrillers will keep you guessing (Kate Morgan, By Death series), and her romantic comedies will keep you giggling (*It's a Dog's Life*, a stand-alone novella; and the Broken Protocols series, starring Charming Marvin, the cat).

Dale honors the stories that come to her—and some of them are crazy, break all the rules and cross multiple genres!

To go with her fiction, she also writes nonfiction in many different fields, with books available on résumé writing, companion gardening, and the US mortgage system. All her books are available in print and ebook format.

Connect with Dale Mayer Online

Dale's Website – www.dalemayer.com
Twitter – @DaleMayer
Facebook Page – geni.us/DaleMayerFBFanPage
Facebook Group – geni.us/DaleMayerFBGroup
BookBub – geni.us/DaleMayerBookbub
Instagram – geni.us/DaleMayerInstagram
Goodreads – geni.us/DaleMayerGoodreads
Newsletter – geni.us/DaleNews

Also by Dale Mayer

Published Adult Books:

Hathaway House
Aaron, Book 1
Brock, Book 2
Cole, Book 3
Denton, Book 4
Elliot, Book 5
Finn, Book 6

The K9 Files
Ethan, Book 1
Pierce, Book 2
Zane, Book 3
Blaze, Book 4
Lucas, Book 5
Parker, Book 6
Carter, Book 7

Lovely Lethal Gardens
Arsenic in the Azaleas, Book 1
Bones in the Begonias, Book 2
Corpse in the Carnations, Book 3
Daggers in the Dahlias, Book 4
Evidence in the Echinacea, Book 5
Footprints in the Ferns, Book 6

Gun in the Gardenias, Book 7

Psychic Vision Series
Tuesday's Child
Hide 'n Go Seek
Maddy's Floor
Garden of Sorrow
Knock Knock...
Rare Find
Eyes to the Soul
Now You See Her
Shattered
Into the Abyss
Seeds of Malice
Eye of the Falcon
Itsy-Bitsy Spider
Unmasked
Deep Beneath
From the Ashes
Psychic Visions Books 1–3
Psychic Visions Books 4–6
Psychic Visions Books 7–9

By Death Series
Touched by Death
Haunted by Death
Chilled by Death
By Death Books 1–3

Broken Protocols – Romantic Comedy Series
Cat's Meow
Cat's Pajamas

Cat's Cradle
Cat's Claus
Broken Protocols 1-4

Broken and... Mending
Skin
Scars
Scales (of Justice)
Broken but... Mending 1-3

Glory
Genesis
Tori
Celeste
Glory Trilogy

Biker Blues
Morgan: Biker Blues, Volume 1
Cash: Biker Blues, Volume 2

SEALs of Honor
Mason: SEALs of Honor, Book 1
Hawk: SEALs of Honor, Book 2
Dane: SEALs of Honor, Book 3
Swede: SEALs of Honor, Book 4
Shadow: SEALs of Honor, Book 5
Cooper: SEALs of Honor, Book 6
Markus: SEALs of Honor, Book 7
Evan: SEALs of Honor, Book 8
Mason's Wish: SEALs of Honor, Book 9
Chase: SEALs of Honor, Book 10
Brett: SEALs of Honor, Book 11
Devlin: SEALs of Honor, Book 12

Easton: SEALs of Honor, Book 13

Ryder: SEALs of Honor, Book 14

Macklin: SEALs of Honor, Book 15

Corey: SEALs of Honor, Book 16

Warrick: SEALs of Honor, Book 17

Tanner: SEALs of Honor, Book 18

Jackson: SEALs of Honor, Book 19

Kanen: SEALs of Honor, Book 20

Nelson: SEALs of Honor, Book 21

Taylor: SEALs of Honor, Book 22

SEALs of Honor, Books 1–3

SEALs of Honor, Books 4–6

SEALs of Honor, Books 7–10

SEALs of Honor, Books 11–13

SEALs of Honor, Books 14–16

SEALs of Honor, Books 17–19

Heroes for Hire

Levi's Legend: Heroes for Hire, Book 1

Stone's Surrender: Heroes for Hire, Book 2

Merk's Mistake: Heroes for Hire, Book 3

Rhodes's Reward: Heroes for Hire, Book 4

Flynn's Firecracker: Heroes for Hire, Book 5

Logan's Light: Heroes for Hire, Book 6

Harrison's Heart: Heroes for Hire, Book 7

Saul's Sweetheart: Heroes for Hire, Book 8

Dakota's Delight: Heroes for Hire, Book 9

Michael's Mercy (Part of Sleeper SEAL Series)

Tyson's Treasure: Heroes for Hire, Book 10

Jace's Jewel: Heroes for Hire, Book 11

Rory's Rose: Heroes for Hire, Book 12

Brandon's Bliss: Heroes for Hire, Book 13

Liam's Lily: Heroes for Hire, Book 14
North's Nikki: Heroes for Hire, Book 15
Anders's Angel: Heroes for Hire, Book 16
Reyes's Raina: Heroes for Hire, Book 17
Dezi's Diamond: Heroes for Hire, Book 18
Vince's Vixen: Heroes for Hire, Book 19
Heroes for Hire, Books 1–3
Heroes for Hire, Books 4–6
Heroes for Hire, Books 7–9
Heroes for Hire, Books 10–12
Heroes for Hire, Books 13–15

SEALs of Steel
Badger: SEALs of Steel, Book 1
Erick: SEALs of Steel, Book 2
Cade: SEALs of Steel, Book 3
Talon: SEALs of Steel, Book 4
Laszlo: SEALs of Steel, Book 5
Geir: SEALs of Steel, Book 6
Jager: SEALs of Steel, Book 7
The Final Reveal: SEALs of Steel, Book 8
SEALs of Steel, Books 1–4
SEALs of Steel, Books 5–8
SEALs of Steel, Books 1–8

Collections
Dare to Be You...
Dare to Love...
Dare to be Strong...
RomanceX3

Standalone Novellas
It's a Dog's Life
Riana's Revenge
Second Chances

Published Young Adult Books:

Family Blood Ties Series
Vampire in Denial
Vampire in Distress
Vampire in Design
Vampire in Deceit
Vampire in Defiance
Vampire in Conflict
Vampire in Chaos
Vampire in Crisis
Vampire in Control
Vampire in Charge
Family Blood Ties Set 1–3
Family Blood Ties Set 1–5
Family Blood Ties Set 4–6
Family Blood Ties Set 7–9
Sian's Solution, A Family Blood Ties Series Prequel
    Novelette

Design series
Dangerous Designs
Deadly Designs
Darkest Designs
Design Series Trilogy

Standalone
In Cassie's Corner
Gem Stone (a Gemma Stone Mystery)
Time Thieves

Published Non-Fiction Books:

Career Essentials
Career Essentials: The Résumé
Career Essentials: The Cover Letter
Career Essentials: The Interview
Career Essentials: 3 in 1